For Sarah, my amazing friend and fellow fan of horror – M.R.

To Bryan (my supplier of beautiful horror books)
and to Maddy (my partner in crime) – T.D.

BIG PICTURE PRESS

First published in the UK in 2023 by Big Picture Press,
an imprint of Bonnier Books UK,
4th Floor, Victoria House
Bloomsbury Square, London WC1B 4DA
Owned by Bonnier Books
Sveavägen 56, Stockholm, Sweden
www.bonnierbooks.co.uk

1 3 5 7 9 10 8 6 4 2

ISBN 978-1-80078-169-6

This book was typeset in Black Madness and Coldstyle Roman.
The illustrations were created in pen and ink.

Edited by Isobel Boston
Designed by Olivia Cook
Production by Ché Creasey

Printed in Latvia

TALES OF THE DAMNED

MATT RALPHS   TAYLOR DOLAN

BPP

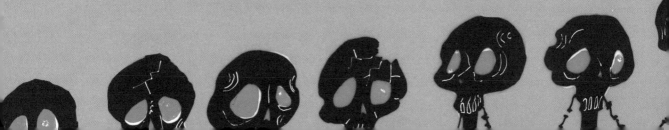

About This Book

We all have fears. Some are logical and shared by most of us: fear of death; fear of pain; fear of losing someone we love. Some fears are less logical, but they are just as real for those who feel them. These are phobias: irrational fears of something that cannot really harm us. And then there are the fears specific to us as individuals: the darkness of the empty house next door; madness and monsters; violence. These fears are as unique to us as our fingerprints, and we suffer them alone.

Terrors, fears and phobias have fed the imaginations of every horror writer who has put stylus to wax, pen to paper and fingers to keyboard for centuries – and they continue to fascinate us to this day. The work of eight of these masters of the macabre – some short stories, some novels – I have retold in this book. For you.

A good horror story elicits a fear response – dread, terror, repulsion – and leaves a lingering sense of unease in the reader's mind. Scary stories have appeared in folklore and mythology throughout history and can be traced back to some of the world's earliest civilisations, including the ancient Egyptians, Greeks and Romans. However, the modern horror genre as we know it today only began to take shape in the late 18th and 19th centuries with the rise of the Gothic novel. Some of the most influential horror stories belong to this style and time. These include Mary Shelley's *Frankenstein* (1818), Bram Stoker's *Dracula* (1897) and the psychologically disturbing short stories of Edgar Allan Poe, published in the 1830s and 40s. Not only did these dark tales (which feature monsters, ghosts, murder and lots of blood and gore) prove incredibly popular at the time, they also set the template for the modern horror genre so many of us love today.

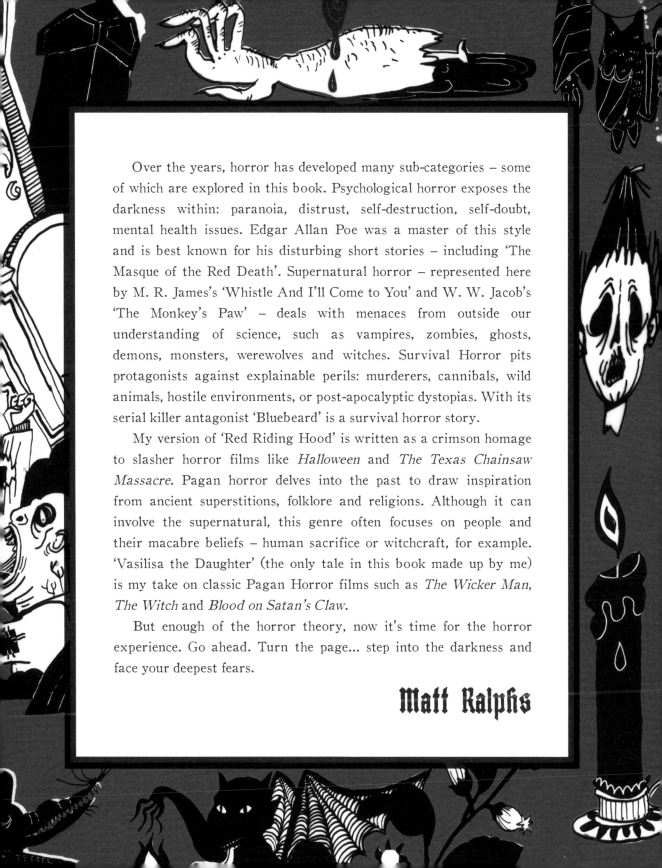

Over the years, horror has developed many sub-categories – some of which are explored in this book. Psychological horror exposes the darkness within: paranoia, distrust, self-destruction, self-doubt, mental health issues. Edgar Allan Poe was a master of this style and is best known for his disturbing short stories – including 'The Masque of the Red Death'. Supernatural horror – represented here by M. R. James's 'Whistle And I'll Come to You' and W. W. Jacob's 'The Monkey's Paw' – deals with menaces from outside our understanding of science, such as vampires, zombies, ghosts, demons, monsters, werewolves and witches. Survival Horror pits protagonists against explainable perils: murderers, cannibals, wild animals, hostile environments, or post-apocalyptic dystopias. With its serial killer antagonist 'Bluebeard' is a survival horror story.

My version of 'Red Riding Hood' is written as a crimson homage to slasher horror films like *Halloween* and *The Texas Chainsaw Massacre*. Pagan horror delves into the past to draw inspiration from ancient superstitions, folklore and religions. Although it can involve the supernatural, this genre often focuses on people and their macabre beliefs – human sacrifice or witchcraft, for example. 'Vasilisa the Daughter' (the only tale in this book made up by me) is my take on classic Pagan Horror films such as *The Wicker Man*, *The Witch* and *Blood on Satan's Claw*.

But enough of the horror theory, now it's time for the horror experience. Go ahead. Turn the page... step into the darkness and face your deepest fears.

Matt Ralphs

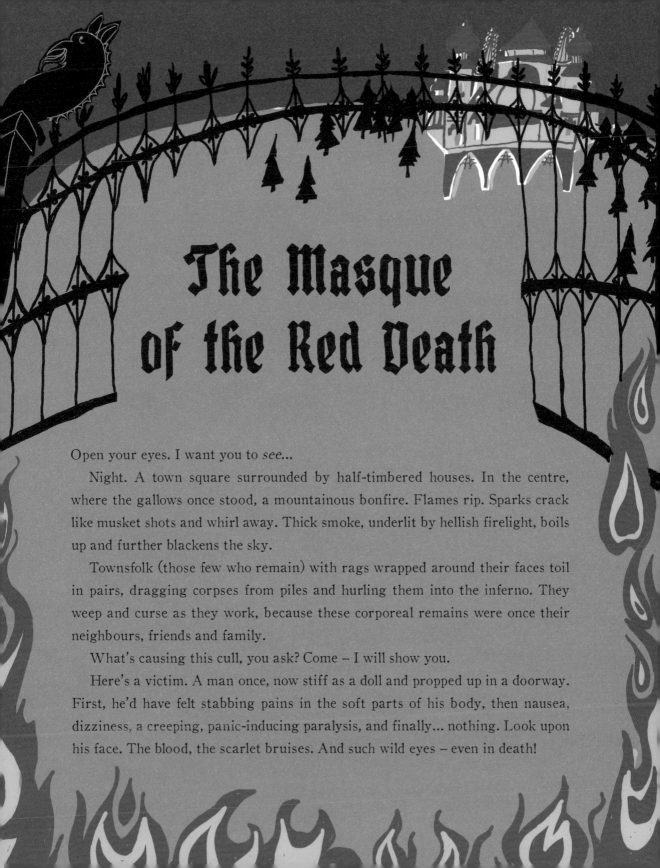

The Masque of the Red Death

Open your eyes. I want you to *see*...

Night. A town square surrounded by half-timbered houses. In the centre, where the gallows once stood, a mountainous bonfire. Flames rip. Sparks crack like musket shots and whirl away. Thick smoke, underlit by hellish firelight, boils up and further blackens the sky.

Townsfolk (those few who remain) with rags wrapped around their faces toil in pairs, dragging corpses from piles and hurling them into the inferno. They weep and curse as they work, because these corporeal remains were once their neighbours, friends and family.

What's causing this cull, you ask? Come – I will show you.

Here's a victim. A man once, now stiff as a doll and propped up in a doorway. First, he'd have felt stabbing pains in the soft parts of his body, then nausea, dizziness, a creeping, panic-inducing paralysis, and finally... nothing. Look upon his face. The blood, the scarlet bruises. And such wild eyes – even in death!

This is the Red Death, a disease that completes its work not in days, or hours, but in minutes.

You'd like to find refuge, I imagine? I know *just* the place! That castle yonder, with towers and ramparts rising high above all this mortal misery. The thousand nobles and knights sheltering within welded the doors shut months ago and not a soul has entered or left since.

But *I* know a way inside. There's always a gap – it's how the dark gets in.

It is Prince Prospero, the ruler of this now half-populated land, who lives there. A happy, carefree man he is. Shrewd too – safely closeted away behind thick stone walls and feasting every night from full larders, while outside his people die in droves. But why should he care about them? After all, they're not rich, or noble born.

Ah, here we are. I told you, didn't I? The gap. Now, let's slip inside, you and I, and see what the jolly prince is up to. These outer halls are dark and abandoned; nothing here except spiders and shadows. The prince and his guests must be deeper inside...

Wait! Is that music I hear? What a merry sound! Come, let's follow the notes... across this courtyard... through this gate... down this corridor... and finally into the Imperial Suite – the innermost and most secluded part of the castle.

The Imperial Suite, designed by the prince himself in his own bizarre style, is compiled of seven capacious rooms, all joined, one to the other, by six gaping doors, but in a way so winding as to quite confound those inside; the rooms flow dawn-east to dusk-west, lit by burning braziers positioned behind stained-glass windows, each in their own colour to match the decorations within; the easternmost room is blue, then comes purple, then green, followed by orange, white, violet... and finally, the westernmost: utterly black.

I will show you *that* room later.

For now, let's stroll east-to-west through these happy six rooms and mingle with the one thousand revellers we find here. My, my! Say what you like about the prince, but he knows how to throw a good party.

Oh, what a poorly chosen descriptor! How could anyone look upon this opulent gathering and think for a moment that 'party' is the appropriate term? A mere *party* would not have scarlet-clad ballet dancers pirouetting on poles high above the throng, or fountains spouting rivers of red wine, or musicians disguised as satyrs and singers as nymphs.

No indeed. This is a ball – a masquerade, no less – of special magnificence held in contempt by the prince against the misery and death held at bay beyond his walls. One thousand people behind one thousand masks, and every design unique! Hooting monkeys, laughing dogs, goggle-eyed fish, leering demons, weeping cherubs, cackling witches: a delirious phantasmagoria, in parts beautiful, terrible, unsettling – and here's that word again – bizarre.

Watch this fêted thousand whirl and dance around us, bathed in the light of each coloured room. Listen to them gossip and prate – their laughter must sound loud trapped behind their porcelain masks. Smell the fat of the roasting pig, the scent of spicy perfume, the tang of sweat. It's hard to spare a thought to the horrors underway outside the walls with all this noise and movement and distraction.

Ah. But now we've come to the last room. The Black Room. Where blood-red light seeps as if from a wound through the stained-glass window and onto walls hung with black velvet tapestries. And while the other six rooms beat full of life, this ghastly place stands empty; not one of the gathering is brave or yet drunk enough to set foot here. But I know you are stout-hearted enough to peer into the gloom and see what lurks against the far wall: an ebony clock with shiny black hands crawling inexorably around a matt black face. Below, a pendulum, from which every swing comes a dull and monotonous *clang*.

14

What will happen when this dreadful clock strikes?

Well, we are bound to find out soon enough, for the night is waning towards its end. In the meantime, let's do what we came here to do and find the prince! Ah, there he is, holding court in jocular fashion and surrounded by his adoring acolytes who praise him loudly for his style, taste and wit, and silently for his unscalable walls, welded doors and laden larders.

Ah, Prince Prospero! All seems so good and fine for you, does it not?

But hark! The dreadful clock speaks! And just look at the effect these doleful midnight tolls are having! The music's faltered, the dancing's ceased and the dying laughter's given rise to a universal gasp of dismay. One thousand masks turn westward as the chimes go on, and on, and on.

Now, this is interesting – unlike every previous hour that's passed this night, the celebrations have not begun anew now that the chimes have stopped.

Instead, everyone – even the bold prince – stands rooted to the spot, faces pale beneath their masks: they've seen another guest, hitherto unnoticed. Follow my gaze. There. See? Standing yonder in the Blue Room, taller by a foot than anyone else and dressed head-to-toe in the raiment of the grave. I don't know about you, but that mask he wears is as convincing a copy of a corpse's shrivelled face as I have *ever* seen, and the speckled blood upon his clothing and the scarlet bruises on his face denote the horror of the Red Death.

Hold still – don't look away. Watch how he glides among the stricken guests! See how they recoil from the dreadful smell! But the prince has gathered his wits, it seems; anger's gained mastery over fear.

"Who dares intrude dressed in such a blasphemous costume? Seize him, my friends! Pull off his mask! I want to see the man who'll soon be hanging from my battlements," he cries.

How disappointing for the prince! Not even his most ardent and obsequious acolytes move to obey his command. Instead, they stand as statues, even as the ghoulish figure passes unimpeded mere inches from the prince and through the purple, green, orange, white and violet chambers, and finally into the Black Room.

"Cowards!"

Tearing off his mask, the prince rushes in furious pursuit. Doesn't the blue light make the dagger he's drawn look as if it's made from ice? Quick, let's follow him into the Black Room, we must see this through to its end.

The figure, a pale shade in the dark, stands, back towards us, staring at the clock. Our royal hero advances, dagger aloft, but the figure turns before the blow is struck and seizes the prince's face with its long-fingered hand. Crimson bruises spread under his skin, red tears flood down his cheeks. The prince's scream tears through all seven rooms and even beyond before he drops, stone dead, to the floor.

And now, *finally*, his acolytes act! With howls of wild despair, they fall upon the figure (mindlessly trampling the prince's corpse as they do so) and claw at his mask and vestments, seeking, no doubt, to kill him with their bare hands. But they fall away, scrambling over one another and crying out in horror as they realise that there is nothing behind that stiff and shrivelled mask, and nothing inside the gown.

And as their vision turns red, and blood spurts from their eyeholes, and paralysis grips their limbs, this feckless thousand realise that their walls, wealth and noble birth are no defence against the Red Death. He is here, with darkness and decay, to claim dominion over all.

Including, my brave companion, you.

Edgar Allan Poe

Although Edgar Allan Poe (1809–1849) was not the first horror writer, he is one of the most important. With his gripping and often grotesque short stories, he elevated the genre to new heights of dread and psychological terror. Truly, no one in the 19th century had ever read anything like it before.

Poe wanted to drag his readers uncomfortably close to human evil. One of the techniques he used was to employ first person narration. In 'The Tell-Tale Heart', we hear the voice of a man trying to convince us that he's perfectly sane. He then explains how – in cold blood and for no real reason – he's killed, dismembered and buried the body of an old man under his floorboards. Then the murderous narrator hears the thumping of the old man's heart rising up through the floor, getting louder and louder, until it drives him so mad he confesses his guilt to the police. Poe's use of first person narration gives the reader an intimate and unsettling view of the character's unhinged mind.

Poe's profound influence on literature did not stop at horror. When he published a short story called 'Murder in the Rue Morgue' in 1841, he virtually invented the detective fiction genre. This blood-drenched and gruesome tale includes many of the classic tropes still used in murder mysteries to this day: the eccentric genius detective; their loyal sidekick who narrates the story; the plodding and mistake-prone police force that serve as an antagonist; and the final climactic scene when the detective reveals the murderer's identity. Without Poe, there'd be no Sherlock Holmes, no Miss Marple and no Jessica Fletcher.

Edgar Allan Poe died in 1849 when he was only forty years old. Fittingly for this master of the macabre, Poe's own death is freighted with drama and mystery. After being missing for about a week, he was found delirious and lying in a gutter in the city of Baltimore. He was wearing someone else's clothes – we don't know whose. Poe spent the next four days in hospital, raving, screaming and hallucinating, until he died. Doctors blamed 'inflammation of the brain', but that's what they often said when the true cause of death was unknown to them.

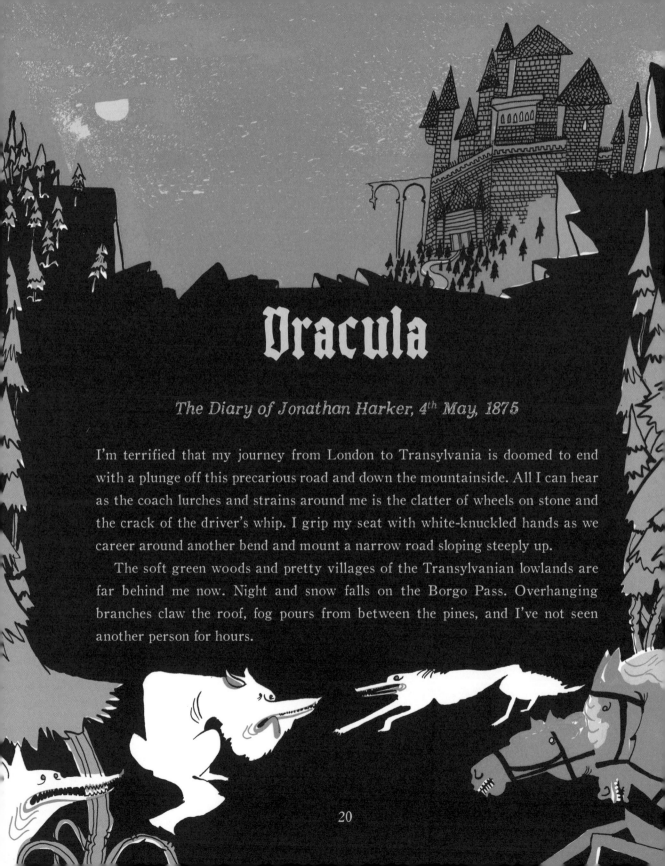

Dracula

The Diary of Jonathan Harker, 4th May, 1875

I'm terrified that my journey from London to Transylvania is doomed to end with a plunge off this precarious road and down the mountainside. All I can hear as the coach lurches and strains around me is the clatter of wheels on stone and the crack of the driver's whip. I grip my seat with white-knuckled hands as we career around another bend and mount a narrow road sloping steeply up.

The soft green woods and pretty villages of the Transylvanian lowlands are far behind me now. Night and snow falls on the Borgo Pass. Overhanging branches claw the roof, fog pours from between the pines, and I've not seen another person for hours.

I poke my head from the window – by *God* this cold nearly takes my breath! – and yell to the driver, "How much further?" He doesn't turn or speak, just lashes his straining horses all the harder. Why this terrible hurry? Are the hounds of hell chasing us? And even as that thought enters my mind, I hear the bone-chilling howl of a wolf.

I nearly fall from my seat as the coach makes a full circle and comes to a rattling halt facing back the way it came. The driver bangs on the roof. "We're here, young Herr," he shouts. "Quickly! Get out!" And the moment my feet touch the ground, he's off and disappearing into the gloom.

"Wait!" I cry uselessly into the freezing night. "Where am I to go?"

Feeling painfully alone, I turn, case in hand, and see the answer to my question.

Castle Dracula, home to the man I've come all this way to meet, rises jaggedly up from the mountain itself and into the moonlit sky. I cross the narrow stone bridge – gathering just enough courage to peer into the chasm below – bang my fist on the iron-studded door and wait, teeth chattering with cold and, I'm ashamed to admit, a touch of fear.

I gaze up at the heavy stone walls, ruined battlements and hundreds of windows letting out not a single scrap of light and think: I'm just a humble solicitor! How did I end up *here*?

I jump at the sound of a key grinding in a lock, and step back as the door swings slowly open. Standing on the threshold with a lantern in his hand is an elderly man garbed in faded silks. He's considerably taller than me, with a frame I would describe as being somewhere between thin and emaciated. This, and the stillness with which he watches me, puts me in mind of a praying mantis. His appearance is, to say the least, disturbing.

He ushers me inside and says "Welcome to my house."

"Count Dracula?"

He bows then takes my hand. His grip is strong and very cold. "Yes, I am Dracula. Come with me. You must be hungry after your long journey."

I follow the Count up a winding staircase then deep into the castle. Dank, unlit passages lead off in all directions and I'm soon quite sure I could never find my way back to the gate without his guidance. At last we pass into a lamp-lit room warmed by an open fire, replete with a supper-laden table – and all my fear (not to mention the cold) melts away.

"Please, eat your fill!" the Count says. "Forgive me for not joining you, but I have supped already."

As I set about an excellent roast chicken, I take the chance to get a proper look at my client. His skin is pale and stretched tight over a domed skull, and his ruddy, thick-lipped mouth looks rather cruel. As he leans close to pour me some wine, I notice (with some disgust) the rankness of his breath and course grey hairs growing from the palms of his hands.

A wolf's distant howl drifts in through one of the windows. The Count smiles, exposing surprisingly long teeth. "Listen," he whispers, "to the children of the night. Such music they make!"

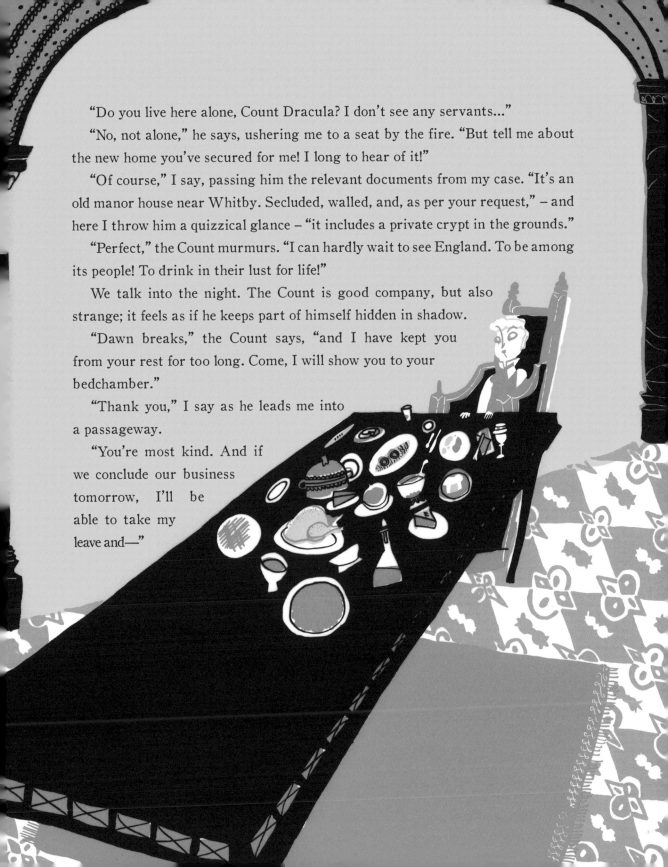

"Do you live here alone, Count Dracula? I don't see any servants..."

"No, not alone," he says, ushering me to a seat by the fire. "But tell me about the new home you've secured for me! I long to hear of it!"

"Of course," I say, passing him the relevant documents from my case. "It's an old manor house near Whitby. Secluded, walled, and, as per your request," – and here I throw him a quizzical glance – "it includes a private crypt in the grounds."

"Perfect," the Count murmurs. "I can hardly wait to see England. To be among its people! To drink in their lust for life!"

We talk into the night. The Count is good company, but also strange; it feels as if he keeps part of himself hidden in shadow.

"Dawn breaks," the Count says, "and I have kept you from your rest for too long. Come, I will show you to your bedchamber."

"Thank you," I say as he leads me into a passageway.

"You're most kind. And if we conclude our business tomorrow, I'll be able to take my leave and—"

The Count stops so suddenly I nearly run into him. "Mr Harker, you are my most welcome guest. I hope you will do me the courtesy of staying longer than a *day*."

"Oh, of course," I stammer, aghast that I might have given offense to my host. "I'd be honoured."

"Splendid! Then you shall stay for as long as it takes for us to become the very best of friends!"

Unsettled by the vagueness of this timescale, I give him a sickly smile as he beckons me into a small, well-furnished bedroom.

"Before I bid you goodnight," the Count says, pausing by the door, "a word of advice. My castle is ancient, full of secrets and dark memories. If you explore, do not delve too far, or too deep. And never try to open a door that is locked. Goodnight. Dream well."

I sit on the bed and let out a shaky breath. Never, in my whole life, have I felt so exhausted and *dislocated* from the world. As for the Count... Well, on reflection, I don't feel altogether sure about him. Not at all.

5ᵗʰ *May, 1875*

I wake to discover I've slept through the entire day! Outside, the sky is deep blue and scattered with stars. I sit up, groggy-headed, and wonder who banked up the fire. A servant? The Count? The thought of him creeping around my room while I was asleep gives me a shiver.

"Come on," I mutter. "A shave will make you feel better."

There's no mirror in the room so I hang my little round travelling glass on the wall by the wash bowl, lather my face with soap and set to work with a straight razor... and nearly cut my own throat when Count Dracula's hand caresses my shoulder.

I whirl round. He's standing right behind me! How could he have crept up on me like that? The mirror shows the door and most of the room! Did he materialise from thin air? I've not even half-gathered my wits when I realise I've nicked my skin and blood is running down my chin.

"Dammit!"

I start looking for something to stem the flow when the Count hisses like a snake and lunges for my throat. Shocked, I push him away, and the moment passes. The Count recovers from whatever madness had taken him, looks away from my wound and hands me a cloth.

"Be careful how you cut yourself," he breathes. "It is more dangerous than you think in this country." Then he slinks away, leaving me shaken and confused.

We meet for supper, and once again the Count declines to eat. Instead he regales me with the history of his land – a long tale of sieges, invasions, fires and famine. He speaks with such enthusiasm it's as if he's recalling these centuries-old events from memory.

"Ah, a new day begins," he says as a dismal grey light seeps through the windows. "I have urgent business, but we shall meet again this evening to continue our journey towards eternal friendship."

Although in dire need of sleep, I decide to explore the castle in the hopes of finding a way out. And so, lantern in hand, I scurry down arched corridors, winding passages and crooked stairways. Shadows leap and slide as I peer into dusty rooms filled with broken furniture and mouldy tapestries. This place is a labyrinth of dead ends, locked doors and maddeningly circuitous routes to nowhere... and after many exhausting hours, my quest has failed.

There's no life here except rats and crows! No warmth! No light! I plunge into an empty chamber and out onto a balcony. This must be the far side of the castle, and the vertiginous drop into the gorge makes my head spin.

I close my eyes and breathe deep the cold air. Flecks of snow settle on my face.

Slowly, slowly, my panic fades. Yes, the Count may be strange and his castle confounding in its design, but I'm not in any *danger*.

Movement from a window a little way below catches my eye. Something pale and round emerges, and I realise I'm looking down on the Count's bald head. Perhaps he wants some fresh air too. But wait...what's this? He's leaning his whole upper body out and placing his hands flat against the stonework beneath the window...

I nearly cry out when he fully emerges. But, instead of plunging to his death, Count Dracula crawls, slowly, insidiously, like some grotesque lizard, down the wall's sheer face. He descends some hundred feet before slithering into some hole or window. How can a man do such a thing? Perhaps he is not a man at all.

6th May

Another long night with the Count has ended, and it took all my willpower to hide my fear and revulsion. Our business is concluded, all papers signed; there's no reason for me to stay, and yet I am compelled to remain. He's disappeared now, as he always does at dawn, leaving me mercifully alone to find the gate. I walk the corridors with purpose, checking every door and sketching a map as I go. After hours of searching, I find a room with a bed and a window overlooking the saw-tooth peaks of the Carpathian Mountains.

Feeling tired and dispirited, I lie on the bed and close my eyes...

The moment I awake I know that I'm not alone. I turn my gaze towards the window and see three young women silhouetted against the ghostly moonlight. They whisper to each other then advance upon me, casting no shadows and making no tracks in the dust. I try to get up, but some irresistible force holds me down on the bed.

My heart races – and not just with fear – as one leans over me. "A tasty fly has landed in our web," she says, licking her lips, "and it's my turn to sup first."

"Be sure to leave some for us," the others reply.

The woman bends her beautiful head closer. Her breath is sickly sweet, her skin grave-cold. Her lips peel away from teeth grown into fangs and, with a soft purr, she lowers her face towards my throat.

I sense something dark rush into the room, and suddenly the Count rears up beside the bed. He grabs the woman – who I've just realised is about to sink her fangs into my flesh – and hurls her from me. The spell that's ensnared me is torn away and I lie quite still, shaking with terror.

Count Dracula's eyes blaze red, as if the fires of hell burn behind them. "How dare you touch him when I have forbidden it?" he intones. "He belongs to *me*!'

The women back away, hissing, snarling, bent like beggars before their master's fury. "But we're hungry," one whines.

"You'll have your turn when I'm done with him. Now go, before he wakes."

"Then are we to have nothing?" another says.

The Count holds up a sack, which moves as if there's something living contained

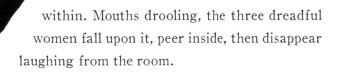

within. Mouths drooling, the three dreadful women fall upon it, peer inside, then disappear laughing from the room.

7th May

I must have fallen unconscious, because when I open my eyes I'm back in my bedroom. What manner of creatures am I trapped here with? I know these blood-drinkers cannot be human. I also know that after what I have seen, the Count cannot let me leave. No doubt he plans to take his fill from my veins then toss me to those women.

If I don't escape, I will never see my darling Mina again.

I must kill the Count or die in the attempt. I have only ever seen him at night, so perhaps he sleeps during the day. Using my map, I return to the room where I saw him crawl outside the castle. I look down at the window and wonder: could that be his bedchamber?

Using every ounce of courage I possess, I slowly descend the wall and drop, feet first, through the window into an unlit passage leading down. Moisture hangs in the air; cobwebs brush my face; things unseen scuttle and squeak.

At last I emerge into a ruined chapel filled with crumbling arches and broken pews. Snowflakes swirl through holes in the roof. I notice that many flagstones have been recently lifted and the earth beneath shovelled into everal coffin-like boxes. I examine each in turn, and recoil when inside one I discover the Count!

He looks dead; unmoving, unbreathing, eyes staring at nothing. And yet, at the same time, he appears transformed into a younger version of himself.

His face is smooth and swollen, his lips full. Most horrid of all are the gouts of fresh blood smeared about his mouth and running in rivulets down his chin and neck. Blood-gorged and bloated, Count Dracula looks like a filthy leech sleeping off its latest feast.

I grab a shovel with shaking hands and hold it blade down over the Count's head. I'm about to strike when he stirs and looks at me with gleaming, malice-filled eyes. In that instant – and may God forgive my cowardice! – I drop the shovel and run pell-mell back up the passage, expecting any moment for him to grab me, draw me close and tear into my throat.

I must escape! Now! I pray for God's mercy and that I survive to warn my country of the demon about to invade their shores.

The Diary of Mina Murray, 4th August

"So," my friend Lucy says, taking my hand, "what do you know about that shipwreck down there?"

"Only what the *Yorkshire Post* printed," I reply. "That it got caught in a storm and ran aground in the harbour."

"Oh, but that's only *half* the tale," replies Lucy with a knowing smile.

Lucy and I are enjoying the afternoon sun in our favourite spot: a bench overlooking Whitby, near the magnificent ruin of Whitby Abbey and its graveyard (which, according to legend, is haunted by a ghostly nun who was bricked up in the walls centuries ago).

"Go on then, tell me," I say.

"Well, apparently it's a Russian ship called the *Demeter,* and it did indeed run aground during the storm, *but*" – and here Lucy's face becomes grave – "not a single soul was found onboard."

"What, no crew? No passengers?"

"No one except the captain."

"Oh. And what does he have to say for himself?"

"Nothing," Lucy replies. "He'd tied himself to the wheel to stop the storm from blowing him overboard, but then mysteriously died. Apparently, the worst thing was the horrified expression on his face."

I gaze down at the *Demeter,* stuck fast on the beach and listing sadly with sails adroop, and wonder what happened to its unfortunate crew. "How awful..."

"And that's not all," Lucy continues. "The hold was empty except for boxes filled with earth, and witnesses saw a huge hound leap off the deck the moment the ship struck and run up the very steps we take to come here. Some say it was a *wolf!*"

"Oh, Lucy! You don't believe *that,* do you?"

Lucy shrugs. "I'm only repeating what I heard."

"Spoken like a true gossip," I chide. "Come on, let's go home – it's getting chilly."

Truth be told, I'm feeling glum and preoccupied. Lucy has recently developed the troubling habit of sleepwalking. Several times during my stay I've found her wandering the house in her nightdress and been obliged to guide her back to bed.

If that weren't enough, I've not heard from my fiancé, Jonathan, for weeks. The last letter he sent was before the final leg of his journey up the Carpathian Mountains. He seemed in good spirits, but I've had no word since then and I'm dreadfully worried.

Dark thunderheads are rolling off the sea by the time we reach Lucy's smart little townhouse, and the wind's getting up. After supper we play cards, and as I listen to the storm baying around the windows, Lucy's absurd notion of a wolf running loose on the streets of Whitby plagues my mind.

I emerge from sleep, tossed on the tides of a howling nightmare. Moonlight shines on the wall clock: it's one o'clock in the morning. I check Lucy's room and my heart sinks when I find her slept-in but now empty bed. A breeze hits me as I scamper downstairs and realise the front door's open and Lucy's gone.

I dash outside without a thought, hoping to see the white-clad figure of my friend – but the street's deserted. Tracing our steps from yesterday's trip, I hurry towards the harbour. As I run up the stairs towards the Abbey, I glance uneasily at the monstrous black bulk of the *Demeter* and cannot shake the idea that it's a herald of something sinister.

I reach the top step and there's Lucy, reclining on our seat as if in a swoon... but my relief dies when I spy a dark and indistinct shape lurking behind her. It looks like the shadow of a tall and lithesome man, and as I watch, it bends down and appears to fasten itself to the side of Lucy's narrow neck.

Lucy's head lolls. Her breathing becomes rapid. She gives a piteous moan that's quickly swallowed by a wet slurping sound coming from the shadow-creature.

Terror and revulsion root me to the spot and it's only when I see poor Lucy grasp weakly at the air that I'm spurred into action.

"Whatever you are," I cry, "leave my friend alone!"

The *thing* looks up, presenting me with a bone-white face, two glowing red eyes and a wave of pure malevolence. I flinch, and in that moment the creature simply disappears.

I dash to the bench, mystified and frightened. "Wake up, Lucy! Wake *up*!"

She looks at me with half-closed eyes. "Mina? Where...?"

"You've been sleepwalking again, dear," I say as calmly as I can. "Come on... Lean on me... That's it."

Somehow, I get Lucy home, and the moment her head hits the pillow she falls fast asleep, leaving me alone and anxious about this night's strange events.

8ᵗʰ August

Oh, how quickly life changes! Only days ago, Lucy and I were happy as skylarks. Now she's bedridden and pale as a ghost. Afflicted by some sickness, she's wasting away in front of my eyes. After a brief examination, the doctor said it's just a prolonged fainting episode and prescribed smelling salts and bedrest.

Ridiculous, pompous little man! He became irate and left when I insisted that Lucy's plight is obviously far more serious. I am my friend's nurse now – feeding, washing, tending to her. I feel there's nothing more I can do. And there's still been no word from Jonathan...

It's midnight and, tormented by worry, I decide to sit with Lucy for a while. I open the door and gasp at the alarming sight of Lucy, fast asleep yet sitting bolt upright, pointing at the window. I draw the curtains and see nothing unusual except a large bat fluttering in circles around a street lamp. I open the window to let in some air, and when I turn around Lucy is lying down again.

9ᵗʰ August

May God have mercy on my most precious friend!

In the few hours since I left her, Lucy's taken a turn for the worse. Her eyes are sunken in their sockets, and her skin's so white I can see the network of veins beneath. If not for her ragged breath and the redness of her lips, I'd think she was dead.

She turns to me and breaks my heart when she whispers, "Help me, Mina, I feel I am slipping away from you..."

"I'll fetch the doctor, and this time I'll *make* him do something."

I fly down the stairs, open the door... and freeze. Standing before me, with one hand raised as if about to knock, is Jonathan. After finding my voice again I cry, "Is it really you?"

"Yes, Mina, it's me," he beams, wrapping me in his arms. "And I can't tell you how long I've dreamt of this moment. But listen" – and his voice becomes earnest – "I must speak to you on a matter of grave urgency."

"As must I."

"Very well. First let me introduce my new friend, Professor Van Helsing." Jonathan steps aside and beckons to a sturdy middle-aged man who, for some reason, is examining the ground under the lamppost.

"Bat droppings," he mutters to Jonathan, before smiling at me and bowing. "Miss Murray. I am glad to meet you. I only wish the circumstances were more agreeable."

I give Jonathan a questioning glance and show them inside. "Your accent, Professor," I say. "Dutch, isn't it?"

"Indeed. I teach at the University of Amsterdam, and that is where Mr Harker found me last week."

"I needed an expert in a very... *particular* subject," Jonathan frowns, "and Van Helsing came highly recommended.' He turns imploring eyes on me. "Mina, we must talk–"

I hold up my hands. "Not yet, Jonathan. I have a crisis of my own," and I tell them of Lucy's rapid descent into sickness; when I finish the men exchange worried glances.

"Miss Murray," says the Professor. "I must examine your friend this instant. Her life may depend on it."

"It's all right, Mina. The Professor's a disease expert, and we can trust him."

I nod and take them upstairs.

"Mein Gott," the Professor says when he sees Lucy lying comatose on the bed.

"What is it?" I say. "What's wrong with her?"

The Professor gently pushes Lucy's head to one side and points to two tiny pinpricks on her neck. "As I feared," he sighs. "The sign of the vampire. These are bite marks. She's lost a lot of blood." The Professor roots about in his bag and produces a rubber tube with needles at each end. "We must transfuse at once. Jonathan?"

He nods and begins to roll up his sleeve.

"No," I say. "Lucy's my friend – nay, *sister* – and I would give every drop of my blood to save her."

"Mina," Jonathan says as the Professor readies his tube, "tell us everything that's happened over the past few days. And afterwards I shall explain what ails poor Lucy, about all my troubles, and my long journey back to you."

They told me everything: about the blood-drinking Count, his ability to take on bat and wolf-form, and how he can only rest in earth from a cemetery in his home country. I believe every word because of what I saw that night at the abbey.

"Our investigation revealed that Dracula hired the *Demeter* to bring him to Whitby," the Professor says, "and that he killed the crew on the way."

"And I let him in to feed on poor Lucy for a second time when I opened the window last night," I say, sick with guilt.

"Most likely," the Professor nods. "But you mustn't blame yourself."

"No indeed," Jonathan says with passion. "Lucy's fate and that of those poor sailors is my fault. If only I'd killed the Count when I had the chance!"

"Absurdity!" the Professor snaps. "Young Jonathan, you faced an ancient and cunning monster alone. It's a miracle you escaped, and you should be proud of your bravery and resourcefulness."

"Well, I'm determined to right my wrong this time," Jonathan says.

I look at Lucy's eyes roving beneath closed lids and the cruel puncture marks on her neck. "As am I. Professor? What will happen to her?"

"She will live, or she will die," he says. "In the meantime, we will give her more blood... and pray for God's mercy."

What a terrible day this has been. My happiness at Jonathan's return is overshadowed by the dreadful things I have learned, and the precarious grip my friend has on her life. We have given her two batches of blood each, but she still looks as frail and corpse-like as ever.

Night's fallen, and when I close my eyes all I see is the hideous white face and burning red eyes of Count Dracula. Monster, demon, *vampire*.

I must have fallen asleep in the chair in Lucy's room because the next thing I know I'm being woken by Professor Van Helsing. His face is wan; Jonathan stands behind him, eyes downcast. "I'm sorry, Miss Murray," he says, "but Lucy is dead."

A wave of grief engulfs me and I scream so hard my throat burns. Jonathan rushes towards me, but I push past and fall upon Lucy. My best friend, who's hardly left my side since childhood, is *dead*.

Eventually Jonathan lifts me away, whispering comforting words that die instantly in my ears. Through a blur of tears I see the Professor bend down to examine Lucy's frozen white face. He mutters something, uses his thumb to lift her top lip away from her teeth, then steps back with a shocked, "Mein *Gott!*"

Lucy's teeth have extended into long, curved, needle-sharp fangs.

"What is it?" I gasp. "What's *happened* to her?"

"I'm afraid your friend was not just food for Dracula," and the fear in the Professor's voice cuts through my grief like a knife. "He's turned her into a blood-drinker too."

"A blood-drinker?" I say. "You mean like him?"

"Yes, a vampire," the Professor replies, "and if we don't act quickly she'll–"

A guttural scream claws its way out of Lucy's gaping mouth, her fingernails tear at the bedclothes, and with hideous swiftness she twists her body into an animal-crouch; we back away as she latches blood-and-hate-filled eyes onto us.

I stare transfixed at this quivering, feral monster that was once my friend.

"*Blood*! *Blood*! *Blood*!" it screeches.

"Stand behind me, Miss Murray," the Professor shouts, brandishing a wooden cross in front of him. The creature hisses and holds up its hand as if warding off a blow. The Professor lunges like a fencer, but the creature springs forwards and crashes through the window.

10ᵗʰ *August*

It is late, and weare crouched in Whitby Cemetery: a walled graveyard packed with crooked headstones and lichen-covered tombs. It is cold. Silver-edged clouds scud across the sky and our breath comes in little puffs of fog.

"Tonight, we're hunters," the Professor whispers, "and we must harden our hearts for the task ahead."

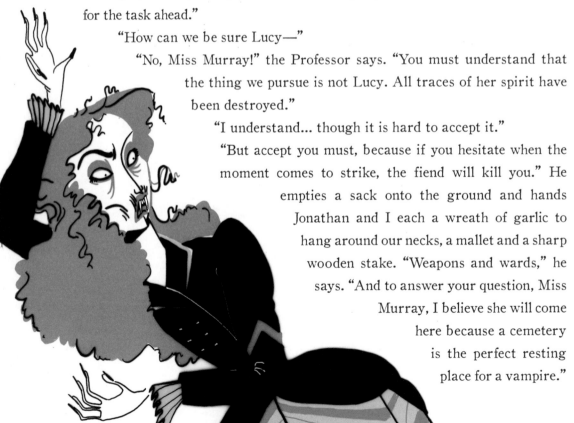

"How can we be sure Lucy—"

"No, Miss Murray!" the Professor says. "You must understand that the thing we pursue is not Lucy. All traces of her spirit have been destroyed."

"I understand... though it is hard to accept it."

"But accept you must, because if you hesitate when the moment comes to strike, the fiend will kill you." He empties a sack onto the ground and hands Jonathan and I each a wreath of garlic to hang around our necks, a mallet and a sharp wooden stake. "Weapons and wards," he says. "And to answer your question, Miss Murray, I believe she will come here because a cemetery is the perfect resting place for a vampire."

We each find a gravestone to shelter behind, and I'm soon shivering with cold and trepidation. I see the haunted look in Jonathan's eyes. I fear he will never fully recover from his ordeal – an ordeal that is far from over...

"Look!" he whispers.

I follow his trembling finger and see the shadow of a figure flit between the gravestones then disappear through the half-open door of a tomb.

"Come," the Professor says. "It is time for action."

I follow as quietly as I can, filled with a tangle of fear and determination.

"The creature's strong," the Professor whispers, "so Jonathan and I will hold it down. And you, Miss Murray, must strike the killing blow."

I nod, and we slip inside the tomb. It's small, room enough only for one raised stone sarcophagus... upon which lies the nightmarish reflection of Lucy.

As the men lean on her shoulders, I place the tip of the stake over its heart, whisper a prayer and bring the mallet down with all my strength. The fiend shrieks, writhes and twists. Crimson foam pours from between its champing fangs.

Another blow and the stake pierces the breastbone with a wet *crack*. Blood bubbles, splashes and spurts. My scream joins the creature's as I drive the stake deeper into its chest.

At last the struggle ends, the tumult quietens, and the blood flow stops.

Breathing hard, we look down on the body that in death – *real* death – looks more like my beloved friend. Choking with grief and guilt, I let the hammer fall from my blood-slick hands and step outside into the moonlight.

The Diary of Jonathan Harker, 10th August

Good God, what a terrible scene! Blood runs off the sarcophagus and patters onto my boots. I move to follow Mina from this house of horror, but the Professor grabs my arm.

"Buck up, Jonathan," he says, "our task is not complete."

I gather my courage, and in what is surely the worst two minutes of my life, we cut off Lucy's head and stuff her mouth with garlic. We're just finishing this grisly task when a scream pierces the night.

I dash outside. Before me, tall and menacing in the moonlight, stands Count Dracula. "You killed my newest child," he bellows, and the force behind his voice presses me against the tomb wall. "And for that I have taken my revenge." He points to Mina, who lies in a shivering bundle at his feet. "She is now mine."

With a cry of fury, the Professor runs forwards, cross held before him; the Count snarls, and in two leaps scales the cemetery wall and disappears. Mina looks up. Her face is grey, her eyes dull, and there are two swollen bite marks on her neck.

16ᵗʰ September

And so I find myself back in Transylvania, where this nightmare began. I'm galloping up the narrow Borgo Pass in hot pursuit of the Count. Snow-clad pines cling to the slopes on my left, the mountain falls away into a ravine on my right.

In front, rides the Professor with a rifle slung over his shoulder. To my side, dear Mina, with a stake and mallet tucked into her belt – and by God, the strength she has shown in fighting the sickness implanted by the fiend makes me love her all the more. But I know she won't survive much longer.

"The only way to save her soul," the Professor told me, "is to kill the Count."

Time's against us. We're desperate to destroy Count Dracula before he reaches his castle and we've been snapping at his heels since we discovered he'd abandoned England – but we've only caught up with him on this, the final stretch. The Borgo Pass.

"There! At last! We have him!" the Professor cries. Snow flies from his horse's hooves as he urges it onward.

Ahead, labouring up the slope, is a cart pulled by two oxen. In the cart bed lies one of the wooden boxes I saw in the castle chapel. Inside, no doubt, lies Count Dracula!

"On, on!" Mina cries, and she flies past with fire and fury in her eyes.

I fall in behind my companions. Cold wind stings my face as we draw level with the cart. The Professor raises his rifle and shouts something in Romanian. The driver looks startled, halts his vehicle and, probably thinking he's being waylaid by bandits, tumbles from his perch and disappears into the trees.

The Professor and I set to work levering up the box lid with our machetes. Mina stands ready, brandishing her stake and mallet. Her face is white, her lips red; she bares them, showing the long teeth beneath.

"Hurry," she says. "We must strike before sunset or Count Dracula will be too strong for us."

With a final effort we break open the lid and cast it aside. Inside lies the Count, deathly pale, staring up at us, his hairy hands crossed across his chest. His eyes shift towards the setting sun, and the hate in them turns to triumph.

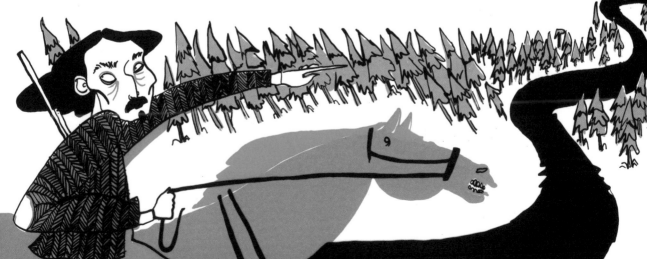

I know we've only seconds to finish him – and yet I cannot move! I'm transfixed by the monster's power, and so is the Professor. But Mina possesses a strength we lack. Standing astride the box, towering above the Count, she screams and plunges her stake deep into Dracula's heart, pinning him like a moth to the wood beneath. His eyes bulge, his limbs thrash, his scream cracks rock and shakes trees.

Spell broken, I swing my machete high and down in a deadly arc, slicing through the Count's neck. Flesh splits; bone cracks; cold blood sprays against my face. And then, before our amazed eyes, his whole body crumbles to dust and is carried off by the Transylvanian wind.

Triumph fills me. It is over! We have rid the world of an evil parasite! After shaking the Professor's hand (what would we have done without him?) I draw my beloved Mina into my arms, and we promise each other a conjoined life filled with love and happiness.

And yet, despite the drama of this final violent ordeal and the intense relief I now feel, I know with surety that my most abiding memory of this day will be the look of utter peace upon Count Dracula's face in the instant of his death.

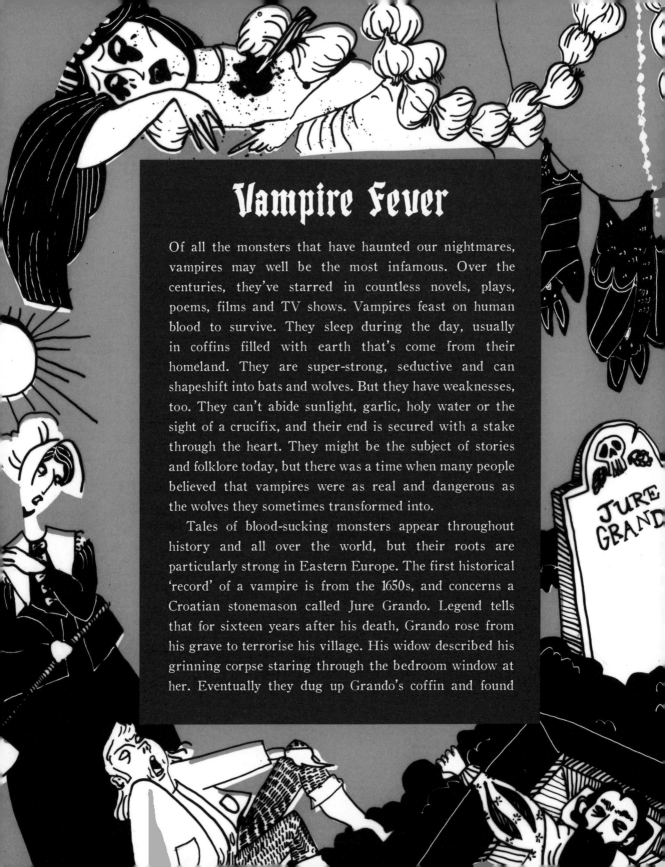

Vampire Fever

Of all the monsters that have haunted our nightmares, vampires may well be the most infamous. Over the centuries, they've starred in countless novels, plays, poems, films and TV shows. Vampires feast on human blood to survive. They sleep during the day, usually in coffins filled with earth that's come from their homeland. They are super-strong, seductive and can shapeshift into bats and wolves. But they have weaknesses, too. They can't abide sunlight, garlic, holy water or the sight of a crucifix, and their end is secured with a stake through the heart. They might be the subject of stories and folklore today, but there was a time when many people believed that vampires were as real and dangerous as the wolves they sometimes transformed into.

Tales of blood-sucking monsters appear throughout history and all over the world, but their roots are particularly strong in Eastern Europe. The first historical 'record' of a vampire is from the 1650s, and concerns a Croatian stonemason called Jure Grando. Legend tells that for sixteen years after his death, Grando rose from his grave to terrorise his village. His widow described his grinning corpse staring through the bedroom window at her. Eventually they dug up Grando's coffin and found

his perfectly preserved corpse inside; he screamed and bled as they sawed off his head.

There is a strong historical link between the belief in vampires and disease. In medieval times (500–1500 CE), when people did not know how deadly diseases such as the plague were passed from one victim to another, they sometimes blamed the spread on vampires. Finding people suspected of being a vampire gave people the (false) comfort that they were taking control of a disastrous situation. People suffering from particular diseases – including porphyria, which can cause skin to blister when exposed to sunlight, and tuberculosis which causes skin to go pale and flesh to waste away – were often suspected.

Before the 19th century, vampires and other blood-sucking creatures were usually bestial and monstrous. This changed in 1819 when British doctor John Polidori's short story *The Vampyre* was published. His vampire, Lord Ruthven, is a handsome, suave and seductive nobleman who preys on beautiful women. Polidori's gothic horror tale proved immensely popular, and it sparked a literary vampire craze. The most famous and influential vampire story is Irish writer Bram Stoker's *Dracula,* published in 1897. Since then, vampires have been a permanent part of our culture... and our nightmares.

The Monkey's Paw

Too late the old man realised his mistake, but having made his choice was just going to have to live with it.

"Listen to that storm," he said, hoping to distract his opponent with some light conversation. "I hope our guest doesn't get blown away on his journey here."

"I'm sure an old campaigner like him has experienced worse than this leaf-loosener," his son murmured, frowning at the chessboard. "Oh-ho! What have we here...?" His face brightened, and he moved his bishop into a deadly position. "Check, and mate!"

The old man groaned. "Not again..."

"Never mind, dear," said the old lady sitting by the fire. "Perhaps you'll beat Herbert next time."

"You're cruel to get his hopes up, Mother," Herbert smiled.

"I wouldn't mind," Mr White said mournfully, "but it was me who taught him the blasted game."

"And now's your chance to teach him how to lose gracefully," Mrs White said.

"You mean, how to lose gracefully *again*!" Herbert laughed.

"I'll lose however I please," Mr White grumbled, unable to keep the smile from his face.

"Badly!" mother and son chimed together.

The three companions turned at a knock on the front door. Mr White threw it open, letting in a squall of wind, rain and murk. "My dear friend!" he cried. "Come and warm yourself by the fire. Here, let me take your coat..."

Mrs White and Herbert rose to greet their guest – a burly man of about fifty, with a military moustache that matched his military bearing.

"Sergeant-Major Morris," Mr White said, "this is my wife, Rose, and my son, Herbert."

After shaking hands all round, Morris sat by the fire and gratefully accepted a large whiskey. "This'll see the chill off," he said. "I'm used to warmer climes, you know."

And for the next hour or two the Sergeant-Major's stories of faraway places, dangerous journeys and dubious deeds flowed as easily as the whiskey, and the White family – who rarely left their county, let alone England – hung on every word.

"Nearly thirty years of adventuring," Mr White said wistfully. "I sometimes wish I'd gone out a bit further into the world."

The Sergeant-Major turned now rather bloodshot eyes upon the old man. "You're best off here," he said. "I envy your contentment," – he held out his glass – "and your home comforts."

"What was it you mentioned the other day, Morris?" Mr White said, pouring another measure. "Something about a monkey's paw?"

"Monkey's paw?" the Sergeant-Major said sharply. "Oh, that... It's nothing... Some might call it magic, I suppose..."

"Sounds intriguing," Herbert said.

"I'm quite curious too," Mrs White added.

Morris eyed her from under his brow. "Consider what happened to the curious cat."

"So? What is it?" Herbert urged.

"Exactly what your father said," Morris replied, drawing something shrivelled and hairy from his pocket. "A monkey's paw."

Mrs White recoiled, but Herbert took and examined it closely. "Look at its fingers," he muttered. "Clenched – like they're holding on to something..."

"What's so special about it?" Mr White asked, peering over his son's shoulder.

"A holy man placed a spell on it," Morris replied. "Three people can make three wishes, and have them granted."

"And have you, Morris? Made three wishes, I mean?"

"I have."

"And did they come true?"

The Sergeant-Major gulped his whiskey (before now he'd only taken sips), knocking the glass against his front teeth as he did so. "They did."

"So why aren't you filthy rich, or King of England or something?" Herbert asked him.

Morris curled his lip. "They weren't those sorts of wishes."

A tense silence fell, broken only by the ticking clock and moaning wind.

"You said 'three people'," Mr White prompted.

"Aye. Three. The man before me had his granted too."

"What were they?"

"The first two I know not," the Sergeant-Major replied. "The third was for death. Then the paw passed to me, and I had my turn."

The Whites were desperate to know more, but something in the old soldier's demeanour warned even callow Herbert against probing further. After a time – during which the ticking clock seemed to get louder – Morris took back the paw and threw it on the fire.

With a cry of alarm, Mr White snatched the smouldering trinket from the flames and dropped it into his half-full glass. It hissed, and the fingers twitched.

"Best let it burn," Morris said.

"If you don't want it anymore, why not give it to me?" Mr White said, drying the thing on his jumper (much to his wife's annoyance).

"I can't. The moment I used up my last wish it stopped being mine. Take it for yourself, if you want, but don't expect my blessing."

"How does it work?"

"You take the paw in your right hand and say your wish out loud." Morris gripped Mr White's arm. "And if you must wish, for God's sake make it something sensible."

The conversation turned to easier subjects, and the monkey's paw lay mostly forgotten on the mantelpiece. Before taking his leave into the cold night, Sergeant-Major Morris drew Mr White to one side. "Have a care with that trinket," he said. "It has a great capacity for... mischief. Goodnight to you."

"I've an idea, Father,' Herbert said, sitting back down by the fire. "Why don't you wish to beat me at chess?"

"I'm actually not sure what to ask," Mr White murmured, picking up the paw. "Seems to me I have all I want."

"Why not ask for enough money to pay off the house?" Herbert suggested. "That'd bring some peace of mind, wouldn't it?"

"I suppose..." And so the old man held up the paw and said, "I wish for two-hundred pounds." Then he let out a shuddering scream and threw it on the floor. "It moved! It twisted like a snake as I made the wish."

"Nonsense!" Mrs White chided. "You've had too much whiskey and excitement, that's all. Come on – bedtime. Don't stay up, Herbert, you've work tomorrow."

"I swear, it really moved..." Mr White muttered as his wife led him up the stairs.

Next morning, the troubled atmosphere from the previous night was forgotten.

"Stuff and nonsense," Mrs White said, clearing the breakfast things away. "How could we have listened to such tall stories!"

"Have faith, Mother," Herbert said. "I'm certain the money will drop on Father's head sometime soon. I recommend he wears a hat for the time being."

Mr White poured himself another cup of tea. "Morris said the wishes were granted in a way that seemed natural, almost coincidental."

"Well, keep your eyes peeled then, Father. I'm off to work."

As always, Mrs White walked her son to the gate and watched until he was out of sight. Upon returning she noted her husband's thoughtful expression.

"You may think me absurd," he said, "but that thing moved, I know it."

"You just think it did," she soothed. "Shall I brew another pot?"

"Go on then."

The morning passed as usual, until Mrs White noticed a smartly dressed man standing outside the gate. Twice he reached for the handle, and twice he retracted his hand. *Strange*, she thought. Then, like a swimmer about to take a dive, he took a deep breath, opened the gate, walked up the path and rapped on the door. She let him in, noting his furtive expression and nervous gestures; the strong impression was that her kitchen was the last place on Earth this stranger wanted to be.

"Mr and Mrs White?" he said.

"That's right," Mr White said. "What can we do for you?"

"I'm here from Maw and Michaels."

"What is it?" Mrs White said. "Oh sweet Lord, has something happened to Herbert?"

"Don't make a fuss, dear," Mr White said, taking his wife's trembling hand. "I'm sure this man's visit is nothing to worry about." And he turned his placid gaze to their visitor and waited.

"I'm sorry," said the man, whose own gaze was flitting everywhere except upon the faces of the old couple. "But your son's been hurt... Badly, I'm afraid."

"Hurt?" Mrs White cried "How? Is he in pain?"

"Not any more." The man looked at his shoes. "He got caught in the machinery."

Mr and Mrs White stood like pale statues as the sinister implication of the man's words seeped into their minds.

"Caught in the machinery," the old man echoed dazedly. "I see."

"Dead?" Mrs White slowly lowered herself into a chair. "But he was the only one left to us."

"The company asked me to convey their most sincere condolences," the man continued, "and even though they admit no liability for the incident, in consideration of your son's years of service, they wish to give you some money as compensation for your loss."

All of the blood drained from Mr White's face. His mouth was so dry he could barely form his next words.

"How much?" he asked.

"Two hundred pounds," came the reply.

After Herbert's funeral, the old couple returned to a silent house. His room they left just as it was, but they kept the door closed as neither could bear to see it. Each drowning in their own grief, they hardly spoke at all.

One night, a week or so later, Mr White woke and found himself alone in bed. The sound of weeping drew his gaze to the window, where his wife sat with her face buried in her hands.

"Come back to bed," he sighed. "You'll get cold."

"Not as cold as my son," Mrs White replied.

Mr White had no words of comfort, no balm to soothe her sorrow, so he lay down to sleep... only to be shaken awake again by his wife.

"The paw!" she cried. "Where is it? You didn't throw it away, did you?"

"No... It's downstairs."

"Oh, thank the Lord!" And Mrs White actually laughed – but there was a wildness in it that made her husband uneasy. "Go fetch it at once," she said, dragging him from the bed.

"But why?"

"Because we still have two more wishes."

Mr White's insides shrivelled with horror. "You can't mean..."

"We can wish our boy alive again," she said, pushing him towards the door. "The first wish came true. Why not the second?"

"Pure coincidence..."

"It was not!" she shrieked. "You wished for two hundred pounds, and now our son is dead!"

"I won't do it," he said, voice quaking. "You didn't see what that machine did to him. I only recognised him by his clothes..."

"You're afraid." She stepped away from him. Her face twisted with contempt. "You're a coward."

Mr White stared at the woman he'd spent most of his life alongside, and saw a stranger. "It would be wrong..." he said weakly.

"Bring him back. I do not fear the boy I nursed."

The man retrieved the paw and brought it back to the bedroom.

"*Wish*," Mrs White said.

Mr White raised the paw. "I wish my son was alive again," he said. And just as before, the grim token squirmed in his hand. He threw it into a dark corner and sank trembling onto the bed. Mrs White returned to her seat by the window and stared intently out with red-rimmed eyes.

Time dragged. The moon hid behind clouds. Cold crept into the old man's bones. The candle burned down until it juddered, sputtered and died. Relieved that the wish had failed, Mr White got back into bed. After a while his wife crawled in beside him.

"I can't bear this darkness anymore," she said in a voice broken with grief.

"I'll get a fresh candle."

Shadows leapt as Mr White struck a match and padded down the stairs. He was about to light another when there came a stealthy knock on the front door. His breath stopped, his blood froze, matches fell from his nerveless fingers. The old man took a backward step, wide eyes fixed on the door.

Another knock sounded, bolder this time, and Mr White fled back to the bedroom and slammed the door behind him. The moon reappeared and cast a ghostly light on Mrs White's expectant face.

"What was that noise?"

"Nothing," he replied, hiding his trembling hands behind his back. "A rat, that's all." He cringed as a barrage of knocks reverberated through the house.

Mrs White, face alight with fevered joy, leapt up and ran for the door; Mr White grabbed her arm. "What are you going to do?"

"It's my boy! He's here! I'm going to open the door."

"For God's sake don't let it in!"

"It?" she screamed. "That's our *son*, and I won't leave him outside." And with a strength neither knew she possessed, Mrs White shook herself loose, shoved the old man aside and flung herself down the stairs crying, "I'm coming, my darling!"

Mr White stood rigid with terror at the furious pounding coming from whatever was waiting for them outside. The scrape of the first bolt being drawn back spurred him into action, and he dove into the corner where he'd thrown the paw and groped frantically about for it in the dark.

"Come down and help me," Mrs White called. "I can't reach the top bolt."

"Don't open it, I beg you," he pleaded, still feeling around on the floor. Where was the wretched thing?

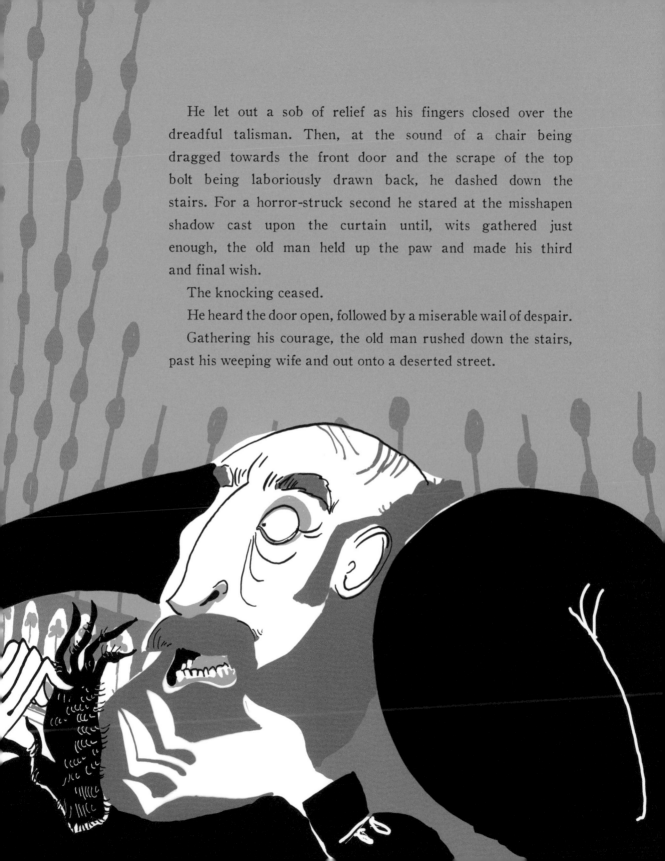

He let out a sob of relief as his fingers closed over the dreadful talisman. Then, at the sound of a chair being dragged towards the front door and the scrape of the top bolt being laboriously drawn back, he dashed down the stairs. For a horror-struck second he stared at the misshapen shadow cast upon the curtain until, wits gathered just enough, the old man held up the paw and made his third and final wish.

The knocking ceased.

He heard the door open, followed by a miserable wail of despair.

Gathering his courage, the old man rushed down the stairs, past his weeping wife and out onto a deserted street.

Crawling from the Grave

There are many things in this world both real and imagined that frighten us, and tellers of scary stories have taken full advantage of this for thousands of years. Whether it's a tale about monsters, murderers or ghosts, horror stories play on our worst fears to chill our blood. So, it's no wonder that death features so often in horror stories. But what if a fate *worse* than death awaits us?

The idea of people returning from the dead to cause mischief for the living has been around for centuries. One of the earliest 'undead' creatures that we know about appears in Norse mythology. The hideous creatures are called *draugr* and they are usually found near their grave or burial mound, jealously guarding treasure against thieves. *Draugr* possess inhuman strength, have the black or dark blue skin of a long-dead body, and carry with them a reek of corruption. Only the bravest of Viking warriors tested themselves against a *draugr*!

Revenants are another kind of undead creature. They appear in European folklore from the Middle Ages – a time when many people believed that the dead really could come

back to life. A *revenant* – which comes from the Old French word meaning 'to return' – is a corpse that rises from the grave to haunt the living. Some *revenants* are brought to life by sorcerers to do their evil bidding. Others want revenge on those who caused them harm in life.

Terrifying tales of the dead have persisted into the modern era. The template for flesh-hungry zombies was laid out in American film director George A. Romero's iconic 1968 movie *Night of the Living Dead*. Romero created a world where the recently deceased come back to life as mindless cannibals driven by a lust for human flesh. With its realistic 'documentary' style direction, gory violence and seriously bleak ending, *Night of the Living Dead* shocked audiences around the world.

Since Romero's ground-breaking work, the undead archetype he devised has firmly planted itself into the public consciousness. The undead star in countless films, books, TV shows and video games. People dress up as them for Halloween and they all know the rules: the undead are mindless, (usually) slow yet relentless, they crave human flesh, their bites cause you to turn, and the best way to kill them (again) is to destroy the brain...

Red Riding Hood

Family, friends and neighbours all called her Little White Riding Hood.

The reasons were obvious, as was their lack of imagination: she was small for her age and always, no matter what the weather, errand or time of year, wore the same white cloak and hood. She did this because she believed it would keep her safe.

Fat chance. It didn't even keep out the rain.

A basket dangled from Riding Hood's arm and inside lay a bottle of red wine and a cake filled with strawberry jam. Riding Hood was well on her way to deliver these treats to Grandma who, despite the inconvenience to her family, still lived deep in the forest.

Far behind, back in the town, the sun cast warm, golden light. But here, among the trees, brambles and briars, darkness reigned, and through its chilly kingdom Riding Hood walked, alone and unafraid.

Unafraid because her mother had made her this promise: "You'll be perfectly safe, my love, just so long as you stick to the path." And so far, her words had proved true. But Riding Hood was too naive to know that her mother wasn't always right, and that luck has a nasty habit of running out.

The beast stalked close behind, downwind and silent, driven half-mad by the scent of human flesh. Lurid perceptions sliced through its brain: screams and gurgles, flesh churning between teeth and tongue, white bone laid bare inside gaping wounds. But cunning instinct overrode its urge to pounce. *Patience, patience* – the beast thought – *perhaps this prey will lead to more...*

Riding Hood was looking forward to some cake and a secret sip of wine from Grandma's glass (the old dear was nearly blind) when she trotted into the clearing. All was as it always was: dappled sunlight shimmered on the grass; above, a green roof of rustling leaves; to the left, a doorless old shed hung with rusty saws, cleavers and bear traps; and ahead, the cottage, little more than a hovel, slump-roofed and sagging.

Sometimes, Riding Hood worried about finding her grandma dead. When her tender imagination envisioned this scene, Grandma was always in repose on her bed, eyes closed, face peaceful, as if in a deep sleep. An easy death, the kind the old woman deserved. Thankfully, on this day, smoke curled from the chimney, meaning Grandma was still alive.

Riding Hood gasped at a radiant carpet of bluebells that had sprung up like magic since her last visit. A bunch of those would brighten up the cottage no end! She'd just about picked a vase-full when an uneasy feeling of being watched crept, spider-like, over her. Her skin prickled, ice ran down her spine. Slowly, breath held, Riding Hood turned to face the forest...

Nothing. No eyes glaring, no goblins leering. And remembering her mother's promise, Riding Hood laughed, shook her head and let her fear drift away like a light breeze.

The beast waited for its prey to turn away before prowling round the back of the cottage. A sniff through the keyhole confirmed that an older meal waited inside; its blood would be thin, its flesh stringy, its bones empty of marrow. But food was food, and the girl would taste extra-sweet after this mediocre first course. A gentle push and the door yielded onto a gloomy room. Against the wall, a bed; licking its drooling lips, the beast rose onto its hind legs, unfurled its claws and loomed over the old woman asleep in it.

Riding Hood looked up from the bluebells when she heard bangs, crashes and cries of alarm coming from the cottage. She smiled, unconcerned, and strolled to the front door, wondering where the best place would be to put the flowers.

"Chasing mice with your broom again?" she called, letting herself in. Through the gloom she could just about see Grandma lying in the bed. "Oh, it's dark! Let me get the shutters..."

Riding Hood gave a yelp as she slipped in something wet. "What have you spilt over here, Grandma?" Experimentally, she slid her boot through the viscous black puddle, then gagged as a smell like warm copper coins filled her nose. It brought to mind the village shambles, of butchery and raw meat...

Feeling suddenly oppressed – frightened, even – by the dark, Riding Hood felt her way to the window and threw open the shutters. Sunlight poured into the little cottage, instantly quelling her unease. Grandma had probably just killed a chicken and dropped the giblets, is all, and so Riding Hood looked into the sink for a cloth to clear up the mess...

Grandma's head, severed raggedly at the neck, glared up at her from a nest of dirty plates. Her dislocated jaw dangled obscenely from two distended stretches of muscle. There was a glistening stump where her tongue should be.

At the moment of dreadful comprehension – which took several long seconds to arrive – Riding Hood doubled over and let go of her breakfast porridge into the sink. When she'd finished, she slowly turned around to take in the room.

It looked for all the world as if an eccentric artist had taken the whole interior of the cottage as a canvas and used only red to express himself. A lake of maroon, thick as oils and scattered with fleshy atolls and corals of shredded skin, shone from wall to wall. Garish arcs of scarlet desecrated the walls and ceiling. Ruby droplets oozed from the rafters.

Riding Hood had stumbled into a bloody tapestry, a crimson hellscape. This scene birthed a question that pierced her fear and bellowed into her quaking mind: If all this gristle and chitling is Grandma, then *what's watching me from her bed*?

The beast leapt, its teeth bared, but the blankets tangled its legs and sent it crashing to the floor. The girl, bug-eyed and screaming, stumbled from the cottage and dragged the door closed behind her. Growling from somewhere deep in its throat, the beast sliced itself free. But it was in no hurry; the girl was weak, slow and leaving a delicious scent to follow, so on its way out it took the time to break open Grandma's skull and lick out her brains.

Riding Hood pressed herself against the back wall of the shed. All she perceived – the sky, the trees, even the bluebells – appeared stained in every hideous shade of red. Her legs felt de-boned; her heart hammered so violently it threatened to tear free from its moorings. Pouring snot and tears, she put her eye to a knothole as a chimeric amalgam of man and wolf emerged from the cottage.

Its belly, pale and scant of fur, was swollen. *Grandma!*

Riding Hood stifled a cry as the beast paused, sniffed the air, then turned its heavy, lupine head towards the shed. Yellow eyes gleamed. Lips slid back from pink-stained teeth to form a malicious grin, and Riding Hood knew she was going to die.

The beast decided – just for kicks – to get to its main course by smashing through the shed like a battering ram. However, before it could do so, it snapped its head towards an unwelcome sound coming from the path. It snarled in frustration at the sight of a man running with purpose towards the clearing.

Riding Hood couldn't believe her eyes when the beast turned tail and bounded away into the trees, or her ears when a man's voice boomed: "Hello? Is someone in trouble? I heard screaming." Sobbing with relief, she tottered out from behind the shed and saw a brawny woodsman carrying an axe. "Well, hello there," he said. "What's got you in such a twist?"

Riding Hood wanted to tell him everything that had befallen her, but the shock of it was so raw all she could do was stare.

"It's all right." He held out his hand. "You're perfectly safe now."

Riding Hood flinched. Those were her mother's foolish words – and lo, something behind the woodsman caught her eye: a loping shadow rushing closer across the bluebells. She tried to shout, but even as the woodsman leaned closer, the monster reared up behind him, a mass of muscle and malice, quivering with anticipation.

A lightning-fast slash turned its claws red.

The woodsman spasmed. He exhibited no pain (not yet), only confusion – as if someone had asked him how many toads he'd eaten that day. He coughed wetly and blood spilt from his mouth. Blue yards of intestine uncoiled from the fresh gash across his waist and slopped onto the ground. Mumbling "*Urgh, ur, ur...*" the woodsman dropped to his knees, dug his hands into the grisly mess and tried to push it back inside.

The beast shoved the woodsman into the offal and stepped on his back.

Oddly, it was this disrespectful act that shook Riding Hood from her terror-induced fugue. With a cry, she snatched up a saw from the shed and hurled it at the beast; a reflexive swipe sent it spinning away.

But Riding Hood was not done yet. Using both hands and rage-fuelled strength, she grabbed a bear trap from the wall and charged towards the beast.

For the thinnest slice of a second, the beast was distracted. Victims, especially soft and tiny ones like this, *never* fought back! A futile gesture, of course, but as the beast recovered, claws angled for the final skewering, it had to acknowledge her courage.

There was a metallic *chomp*, and it was suddenly impossible to take another step. The beast looked down and saw the bear trap on its leg, serrated jaws snapped tight.

And then the pain hit.

Riding Hood scrambled away on her rump as the beast clawed desperately at its ankle. It howled and gnashed its teeth, then turned hate-filled eyes onto her. Shaking with panic, she picked up a rusty old cleaver.

The beast, bleeding badly, bent low and dragging its wounded leg behind it,

staggered towards her; she got a whiff of its animal stink, a blast of hot breath on her face... until an unseen force jerked it backwards. Gasping for air, the Beast reached for the loop of rope around its throat, before falling hard onto its back.

The brave woodsman lay beneath, straining to keep his slippery noose around the beast's neck. Taking this precious chance, and with a vision of Grandma in her mind, Riding Hood set about her enemy with the cleaver.

Edged metal and unfettered fury rained down until the beast's head was nothing more than a meaty ruin. The cleaver slipped from Riding Hood's trembling fingers and she bent down to whisper "thank you" to the woodsman just before he died.

A few hours later Riding Hood emerged forever changed from the forest, with her cape, hood and soul stained red from her battle with the beast.

The Dark Fairy Tales

Everyone has a favourite fairy tale. These classics are often the first works of fiction we hear as children – perhaps told to us at school or at bedtime before the lights are turned out. Packed full of iconic archetypes such as trolls, giants and witches, set in evocative locations like forests and rambling castles, and drenched in themes of love, death and transformation, is it any wonder that fairy tales embed themselves deeply into our consciousness?

Fairy tales have been told for centuries, but the modern versions we know so well are very different to the original, much darker stories. They began life as folk tales and they have been told, retold, adapted and changed so many times that it's hard to know exactly when they originated. We do know that each tale had an important life lesson: don't stray from the path; don't go into the woods alone; beware wild animals. These sinister stories served as a reminder to children and adults alike that the world could be a dangerous place.

It was German brothers Jacob and Wilhelm Grimm who popularised fairy tales with their book *Children's and*

Household Tales, published in 1815. They adapted the stories, removing much of the original violent and sexual content, and changed the tragic endings to happier ones; this gave them a broader appeal – and ensured their books sold more copies!

It's easy to understand why the Grimms edited the stories for children. In one early version of Red Riding Hood, the wolf not only devours the grandmother, but he also leaves some of her flesh and blood out – which the unwitting girl actually eats! Far from being saved by the brave huntsman, Riding Hood is also consumed by the wolf. However, a different version has Riding Hood use her cunning to escape from the wolf's predations...

Early versions of Snow White are more violent too. When the evil Queen sends out the huntsman to kill Snow White, she also orders him to cut out the girl's liver and lungs so she can eat them. Yet more cannibalism... In the end, as punishment, the Queen is forced to put on a pair of red hot shoes and dance until she drops down dead; that bit of entertainment takes place at Snow White's wedding to the handsome prince.

Fairy tales are underpinned by so many rich themes (including love, death and revenge) that they are just as powerful and inspirational today as they were centuries ago.

Frankenstein

The Diary of Victor Frankenstein, Ingolstadt, Germany, 1793

I'm meeting my best friend for a nightcap, and I must pretend that this evening has been just like any other. He'll ask, "What have you been up to?" To which I'll reply, "Studying for tomorrow's anatomy lecture. The usual." And because I am an excellent liar, and dear Clerval is so trusting, he'll believe every word.

Ordinary people would feel shame and disgust for the things I've done tonight. Not to mention the things I'm *about* to do. They'd curse and spit on me, exile me forever. But what do *they* know? They, who view life's canvas so close, that they fail to see the wondrous picture beyond the portion trapped within the frame.

But I am not constrained by such petty limitations.

I pause at the entrance to the bierkeller. I should probably change my clothes before going inside. Get this graveyard stink off me. But it'll be smoky and boozy in there, which will mask the smell... Besides, I want to get this over with so I can return to the laboratory and finish my work.

Just between us, I think tonight might be when my long and grisly labours will at last bear fruit – and if they do, the world will never be the same again. Feverish with excitement, I heft my leather bag and plunge inside.

Aha! There's Clerval – in the corner as usual, and looking pensive; I order two beers and take them over.

"Victor!" he cries, getting up and shaking my hand. "I was starting to think you'd forgotten about me."

"As if I would."

"You do sometimes," he says with a raised eyebrow. "Is that for me?"

I hand him his beer and sit opposite. "Sorry. Got lost in my books."

"Ah – anatomy studies," Clerval says disapprovingly (he's a literature student). "The art of demystifying the miracle of life. Which bit are you laying bare now?"

"The heart," I say, glancing down at my bag. "And life isn't a miracle, it's simply science."

"It's God's domain," he sniffs. "And it doesn't do to go poking around in it."

I assess him over the rim of my glass. Does he suspect something? Does he have any clue about the dark deeds I've undertaken these past two years? *Does he know what's waiting for me back in my lab*?

No. It's just Clerval being intellectually prudish and old-fashioned, and much as I love him for his loyalty, his mind does not fly as high as mine.

"I received a letter from Elizabeth today," Clerval says, looking a bit awkward. "She says you've not written to her or your family for months."

"I've been busy," I mumble.

"They're worried about you, my friend. As am I. You're shabby, thin as a rake and look exhausted. Shattered, even. Do you ever sleep?"

"Of course," I lie. "Like a babe, every night."

"Well, it doesn't look like it."

Instead of slamming my fists onto the table and demanding Clerval mind his goddamn business, I smile and say, "Don't fret – I've been preoccupied, that's all. I promise to be a more attentive son, fiancé," – I raise my glass to Clerval – "and friend very soon. I just need to finish something first."

It's midnight by the time I get back to my rooms. I don't feel at all well. Thanks to Clerval, I've a mixture of guilt and beer swilling around my stomach – the

💀 69 💀

last things I need given the challenging task ahead. I'd like to postpone, but the contents of my bag will not stay fresh for long.

No. It must be tonight. It must be now.

I lock and bolt my door and hurry up the narrow staircase to my attic laboratory; rain begins to patter on the windows as I light the lanterns. A storm's coming. How appropriate.

I place my bag with a sort of reverence on the cutting table. Is what's contained within really the last piece of this glorious puzzle? Or another soul-hobbling dead end? We shall see. I glance up at the high steepled ceiling and, not for the first time, I am reminded of the family church back in Geneva and my most abiding memory of that place: my mother's funeral.

I take a calming breath and survey my chapel of creation: my books on anatomy, medicine, alchemy and dark magic; my demijohns of chemicals, alkalis and acids; my vats of cloudy preservatives filled with organs and body parts (all stolen, or purchased in dark alleys from unprincipled undertakers and morticians); the humming electric devices drawing power from towering voltaic piles; a board pinned with writings, drawings and a print of Michaelangelo's 'Creation of Adam' – and in the centre of the room, shrouded with a sheet, a raised ceramic tank the size and shape of a large bath.

And within? My legacy.

I remove the sheet with trembling fingers and, with a queasy mixture of adoration and fear, gaze through pond-coloured fluid at the naked figure floating beneath. Unmoving. Dormant. *Dead.* I twist a handle; the fluid gurgles away, slowly revealing a corpse – or, to be accurate – an amalgam of corpses, spliced, grafted, interknitted.

I take a moment to admire my handiwork. The body is perfectly proportioned. The skin, although originating from many different men, seems like one organ with nary a nick or gap to betray its piecemeal construction. The surgical attachments – hands-to-wrists, limbs-to-trunk, head-to-neck – are smooth and neatly sewn. Eyes closed. Features peaceful. Hair black and long.

"Beautiful," I murmur, "but not yet complete."

I dig my fingertips into a near-invisible slice in the breastbone and gently open the left-hand side of the ribcage. Nestled between a glistening pink lung, a sullen grey liver and a mess of dangling pipe-like artery ends lays the final fleshy gap, waiting to be filled.

Now, fresh human hearts are heavy *and* slippery, so I use both hands to transfer it from my leather bag to its new home. I sigh with relief – it's a perfect fit! – take needle and thread and bend with a will to this final momentous task...

'Tis done! The heart is in place, the chest sealed up and sewn, and my life-giving elixir – years in the making – has been tubed into my creation's veins. The electric wires are connected and all I need do is throw this switch.

Rain batters the windows. Lightning flashes. Thunder rolls. If I were a superstitious man, I'd think God was angry with me. And yet it is *I* who am angry! Angry that I've had to do my work in secret. Angry that society has constrained my genius and made me a criminal. Angry that this epochal moment, this miracle wrought by me, is taking place in this miserable attic instead of before an admiring audience of the great and good.

I throw the switch with a vicious downward thrust.

The machines and voltaic piles hum, thickening the air and making the hair on my arms stand up; I can actually feel the power flowing from metal into flesh! I gasp as my creation's fingers twitch. Then my heart fills with joy as he opens his mouth and inhales a rasping lungful of air.

He's alive! He's *alive*!

I'm about to attend him when he begins to thrash. Thrash and flail. Thrash, flail and scream. Dear God, what a sound: full of pain and fear. He batters his head into the ceramic, leaving bloody smears behind. I stare in mounting dread as his skin gets tight and begins to swell. My stitches, so carefully made, pull apart and snap. The seams between each appendage widen, revealing the fat, flesh and muscle beneath.

And then it opens its eyes and turns them upon me. Yellow, watery, brimming with sensations it cannot hope to comprehend, and all my joy curdles to disgust for this slithering, burbling monstrosity. I stumble away, sending a standing shelf of glassware crashing to the floor. The creature tumbles from the tank and begins to crawl towards me, belly down, head up, still shrieking.

It lays a hand on my boot. Shaking with horror, I kick its upturned face and flee into the night.

Geneva, Switzerland

I remember little of what happened next. I must have wandered the alleys of Ingolstadt for hours until, like a migrating bird driven by instinct, I ended up on dear Clerval's street. He found me next morning, collapsed and shivering on his doorstep. And, true to his character, he took me in and tended to me.

Those following weeks were a torment. Body already weakened by self-neglect, I fell into a desperate fever; Clerval has since told me he feared several times I would die. I raved and cried out in the night, plagued with images of a looming figure standing at the foot of my bed, and filled with bitter disappointment that my high-flying dreams had, like Icarus, come crashing to the ground.

After several months of this agony I came back to myself a bit, and Clerval accompanied me home to Geneva. And there exists no more soothing balm to my troubled soul than being back in the family mansion and in the care of my father, younger brother William, and Elizabeth, the love of my life since I was a boy.

I'm happy to report that my strength is returning. I walk the grounds; I take my repast; I even sleep sometimes. I think less and less of the *creature* now (the best I can hope for is that it found some dark place in which to die) and more of my next attempt.

I must certainly account for the physical swelling caused by the animating process. Looser skin, longer stitches... And for the initial violent physical reaction: restraints around the ankles, wrists and neck... Perhaps a sedative. Or a weaker specimen to begin with... A child, perhaps?

I have much to consider. I must ask Father for pen and paper, lest I forget my best ideas!

I close my notebook with what I hope is not too obvious haste when Elizabeth, William and his nanny, Justine, burst into my bedroom; William, as is the little fellow's habit, runs over and gives me a hug.

"Justine and me are going for a walk up the mountain," he says. "Will you come with us? I want to find an edelweiss flower for Lizzie to wear in her hair."

"We won't be going *that* far up the slopes, William," Justine sighs. "My legs are far too old."

"Then I shall go alone," William earnestly expounds, "for I do not fear the harsh cold and hard rocks of the mountains!"

"Well, I do," Justine says. "We'll stick to the foothills, if you don't mind."

"There're lots of flowers in the meadows," I say. "Cowslips, snowbells, primroses. More than enough to make Elizabeth a pretty garland."

"Oh, all right," William says. "But you will come with us, won't you, Victor?"

"Your brother needs to rest," Elizabeth says, "but he'll be strong enough to accompany you on a mountain expedition soon, I promise."

"We'll be back before supper," Justine says, taking William's hand.

"Goodbye," I say. "Have fun!"

Elizabeth sets up a little folding table between us and sets out the chessboard. "I'm determined to win today."

"Oh, really?" I say to her, masking a smile. "And how long is it we have been playing together?"

"Since we were about six, I suppose."

"And in all that time, have you ever beaten me?"

"I'm not sure..."

"Never."

Elizabeth huffs and, as always, opens with a knight move.

"You rush," I say, "and make the same mistakes over and over."

"I lose concentration" – and she glances sharply up at me – "because you take so long to make decisions."

I sigh and lean back in my chair. "We will be married soon, Elizabeth, I swear–"

"But when?" she cries, cheeks flushing with passion. "We've been engaged for *two years,* Victor!"

"When I've completed my work," I say, eyes straying to my notebook. "You know about my studies..."

"Is that more important to you than us? The life we could be sharing?"

I grab her hands and say something that is not quite a lie: "Nothing is more important to me than our love. *Nothing.*"

We finish the game (I win) in a rather icy atmosphere, but all I have to do is wait her out; Elizabeth has such a warm soul she's defrosted by the time we take an evening stroll around the garden. Father and Clerval join us by the fountain, just as the sun pierces itself on the highest alpine peak.

"It does me good to see you recovering so well, Victor," Clerval smiles.

"We were all so worried," Father adds. "How could you have let yourself get into such a state?"

"He's promised to look after himself better from now on," Elizabeth says, slipping her arm through mine.

Father checks his pocket watch and frowns. "It's getting late. William and Justine should be back by now."

"Weather's closing in too," Elizabeth says, nodding to an ominous pile of clouds gathering on the horizon.

"I'm sure they're fine," I say. "If they're not back soon, I'll go and look for them."

Neither returned, and so I find myself, hours later, desperately worried, separated from the search party, and striding through the woods with nothing but my overcoat to protect me from the pouring rain, and a lantern to stave off the dark. My throat is sore from shouting, but still I call out.

"William! Justine! Where are you? If you can hear me, please come towards my voice."

Arm raised against the lashing wind, I emerge into a clearing. The ground ahead rises steeply to form a rocky promontory that's perhaps thrice my height. A huge figure stands at the apex, face hidden under a wide-brimmed hat and holding two duffel bags, one in each hand. It's broad of shoulder and horribly strong, but... *wrong* in form: lumpen, misshapen, misaligned. Even at this distance I sense its base charisma; the creature puts me in mind of some ruined demigod, spat forth from the underworld with dark intent.

Lightning flashes, and for an instant I see the hideous face of my creation leering down at me. There's no fear in it now. No confusion. No pain. Just malice, directed like a bullet, at *me*.

Dread flops in my stomach like a dying thing.

How can this be? How did it survive? And what dread motivation has driven it back into my orbit? Before I can speak, or pick up a rock, or run, the fearful golem raises the bags into the air and drops them over the edge. They hit the ground in front of me with heavy thumps, and I realise they're not bags at all, but the broken dead bodies of William and Justine.

I cry out in grief and rage and start towards my enemy but, with a final triumphant grin, he jumps from the rock face and disappears into the darkness.

Everyone thinks I suffer the same grief as them. But they're wrong, because mine is mixed with so much guilt I fear I'll drown.

You find me sitting on the front row of a packed church, staring with sore eyes at William's coffin. Father's utterly broken and has barely spoken since I returned home bearing his youngest son's limp body. Realising it was murder, Clerval immediately gathered all the servants and organised a manhunt, but I instinctively knew the creature would never allow itself to be caught.

In the end, though, they *did* catch someone. A beggar of barely sound mind sleeping in a nearby barn. Even now he languishes in a cell awaiting trial; everyone believes he's the killer and is destined to hang. I know otherwise, of course, but am powerless to help him. After all, who'd believe my story? And even if they did, as the killer's creator, they might hold me responsible.

But I am not. The creature is to blame! And as I sit listening to the priest, the same question rolls around my mind: Why did it decide to bring death to my doorstep?

There are reminders of my brother everywhere – his cup, a discarded toy soldier, his book of pressed flowers – and they all widen the wound in my heart. Each day I try to escape by walking ever further into the mountains, but my grief never loosens its grip.

It's a miserable, drizzly day, and there's a low-lying fog obscuring the foothills below this lofty vantage point. I feel lost. Alone and wretched in an endless sea of sorrow. I harbour no more dreams of creating life from death. Clerval was right – it's God's domain. Not to be meddled with.

But wait... What's that? A figure bounding towards me, leaping from rock to rock with a speed and agility far beyond an ordinary person. It's him! Hatred courses through my veins; my mind fills with thoughts of murder. As it closes, I see bitter emotion etched into every scar on its dead flesh-face.

"You dare seek me out after what you've done?" I cry as the creature's shadow falls across me. "Monster! Murderer! Come closer still so I can choke the life from you!"

"I expected this reception from thee," the creature intones, gazing down at me with baleful eyes. "After all, the hardest lesson I have learned in my short and pathetic life is that all humans hate the wretched. And am I not the most wretched thing you have ever beheld?"

His eloquence amazes me (what was I expecting… guttural noises and grunts?), but not as much as the doleful sadness in his voice. It is a tortured sound.

"I see an abomination," I hiss in anger. "A demon. An inverse reflection of all that is good and kind."

"And why do you think that is so?" He stares hard at me for a long moment before continuing. "My first experience, after being dragged unwillingly into this world, was rejection by the first living creature I beheld. You. And so it has been with all people ever since. I've been beaten, hated and hounded not through any fault of my own, but solely because of my appearance.

I was forced to hide in the wilds and lament alone my miserable existence. I sought solace in the beauty of nature, the radiance of the moon, the warmth of the sun, but in the end nothing eased my boundless despair. And so I turned my mind and infinite capacity to hate onto you, who left me alone and unprepared for this cruel world." He regards me shrewdly. "You probably wished that I'd died, didn't you? Your own child."

"I did," I whisper. "And I still do."

His face twists into a bitter

smile. "Yet you made me hardy enough to survive all these travails, and clever enough to seek you out and make this demand."

"What demand? Waste no more of my time, demon, and tell me what you want."

"You will create for me a female, a mate, a companion, who instead of shunning and hating me like your kind does, will give me love – that precious thing for which I yearn from the bottom of my broken soul. Do this for me, your creation, and I will disappear with her into the wilderness and trouble not you, nor your family ever again."

"And if I refuse?"

His eyes narrow. "Then I shall glut the maw of death with the blood of your remaining loved ones," he growls. "Remember, Frankenstein, you may be my creator, but I am your master. Do my bidding... or reap my revenge."

I need seclusion to carry out the monster's dread desire, so I've leased a nearby castle from Baron Brennenburg, an old family friend who abandoned it years ago. Standing atop a hill, partially ruined and surrounded by trees, it suits my purpose well. Dismantling and transporting my laboratory from Ingolstadt took weeks, but everything's set up now in the Great Hall – a draughty and depressing place.

Desperation to be rid of the creature drives me well beyond my already considerable limits; I work every day until my strength is utterly spent and it's all I can do to drag myself to a makeshift bed in the corner and collapse into fitful sleep.

I rarely go home. I simply cannot face them. And I know *he* is near. I never see him, but I feel his malignant gaze on me, watching, waiting, ensuring I'm pursing my end of the bargain without delay or distraction.

My contacts in the body-snatching trade have furnished me with the raw materials I need (including, God forgive me, poor Justine's mouldering corpse) and I am deep in the bloody and laborious process of forming a female that will rise from oblivion into waking life. A mate for my monster.

And to think the idea of defeating death, of bringing back those we love (Mother...) once seemed so righteous to me!

But it's true what they say: the road to hell is paved with good intentions.

Elizabeth looks beautiful, even in black.

I've torn myself away from my ghastly labours to spend the morning at the manor. Damn my soul, but I'd rather be elbow deep in gore than here, among the people who suffer so for my creation's sins.

She stands a few paces away, staring towards the distant mountains; for my part I sit on the fountain wall, the very picture of forlornity. I feel this distance between us as clearly as the cool spray through my shirt, and my heart breaks even further.

"How's Father?" I venture.

"Why don't you go see him for yourself?" she replies. "It might ease his pain a little to spend time with his one remaining son."

I flinch at that. "I'll go up presently..."

She rounds on me, her face a mix of anger and confusion. "Where do you go for days on end that's so much better than being here, with we who love you? Who *need* you?"

"I've told you – I walk the mountains because I must be by myself for a while." That's a lie, and it comes easily. "My grief... for William... it just won't lift." That's the truth, and it comes hard.

"I understand," she says, kneeling before me. "We all share your sadness, Victor. But believe me, it's easier to bear together. Won't you come back to us? Please?"

I look her in the eye. "I will soon. I promise."

Partially mollified, Elizabeth sits by me and slips her arm through mine – a simple gesture that nearly reduces me to tears. "Let's marry," I declare, borne along on this sudden rush of emotion. "Next Saturday – no later! Life is precious

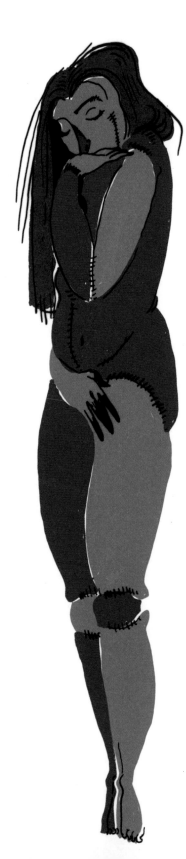

and we must make the most of it, don't you think?"

The happiness on Elizabeth's face conveys her answer with more eloquence than words could ever allow.

Tomorrow I am to marry the woman I've loved my whole life, but instead of celebrating, I'm in my lab, staring down at this, my second abomination. She – *it* – lies on the slab: a stitched-together nightmare with a face that even without animation is the very definition of vile.

Will the creature find this unholy chimera pleasing? Will he, like me, recoil from its chilly flesh? Abhor the mould covering its skin? Be repulsed by the stink of corruption? I have no idea. But even as I open the valves and allow my elixir to flood its veins, more pressing worries pluck at my nerves.

The creature promised to live out its life in the wilderness and never trouble me, my family or any other human again. I believe him. If I didn't, I would never have agreed to this foul undertaking.

They'll never breed (I've made sure of that), but what if his mate decides she's not morally bound by his oath, and finds the notion of living in solitude unappealing? What if she loathes him on sight? And what if she turns out to be an even more malevolent and hateful creature than he? One who delights in murder and revels in violence? I shudder to think of the mayhem she could cause if she strikes out on her own and the toll that would take on my already wounded soul.

Oh, wicked God! Why have you cast me, who had

such boundless potential, as the modern Job and cursed me with so much misery?

Movement catches my eye and I see the creature framed in a high window, looking down with a victorious grin onto its new companion. I am struck with a lightning flash of clarity – *I cannot do this!* – I grab a cleaver and begin to hack. Flesh splits, bones snap, brains splatter, and in seconds I've reduced a being who was only a lever-pull away from sentient life into a formless, dripping mess.

I clamp my hands to my ears as a deafening cry of anguish echoes around the hall. The creature leaps from its perch and next moment I'm pinned by the throat, feet dangling, vision filled entire with his wrathful face.

"You killed her!" he bellows. "She would have made my desolate life worth living!"

"Yes," I gasp, "and I'd do it again, a hundred times!"

"Liar! Worm! You dare defy me?" He is mad with rage.

"I do. Kill me, if you wish, but I will never bring another like you into this world."

"I will not kill you, for that would end your suffering." He draws me close and presses his brow against mine. "From this moment, my only goal is to compound your misery till it surpasses my own. I shall pulp your heart, Victor Frankenstein, and grind your soul into powder."

And with those dread words, he drops me and runs from the hall. I crawl to the window, just in time to see him disappear into the trees, heading apace towards the distant lights of the manor.

I open the smashed front door and, with quaking heart, creep into the hallway. All the lamps are lit – evidently wedding preparations were still being made when the creature descended. The first thing I see is poor Clerval, lying on his back, head at a hideously unnatural angle, with a poker still gripped in his hand. Beyond him, one of the maids, crumpled lifelessly in a corner.

I nearly collapse when I find Father dead in his bed, with the indents of the creature's fingers still impressed in the pillow covering his face. I scour each room, but there's no sign of Elizabeth or the creature, just more and more murdered servants.

I sink to my knees and weep until my mind realigns and thoughts begin to form clearly again. Everyone is here except Elizabeth, so perhaps she's not dead. Perhaps he's merely kidnapped her – and if she's alive, she can be rescued!

Holding this flickering hope like a candle in a storm, I stagger into the garden and sit by the fountain – the last place I saw my beloved. Feeling sick and feverish, I turn round to splash some water on my face. Elizabeth, dress billowing around her, stares up at me from the bottom of the fountain – eyes wide, lips blue, narrow neck ringed with bruises.

I drag her from the depths and hold her close. And even as my tears mingle with the water streaming from her hair, I spy the creature watching me from the shadows.

"Wherever you go, I shall find you, demon!" I cry, as he retreats into the night. 'Even if it be to the ends of the Earth, I swear I shall hunt you down and kill you for what you've done!"

After laying the bodies of Clerval, Father and Elizabeth together, I pack a bag with essentials and with single-minded purpose: to set off after the monster.

And so began our epic chase – two enemies bound by mutual loathing. Days turned to weeks, and weeks to months. For a year I've followed his trail, ever northward across the continent, into Scandinavia and across the sea to the Arctic wastes. He leaves me markers, messages, even bundles of food, egging me on in my endless pursuit, but always staying just out of reach, taunting me, revelling in his protracted revenge.

I'm painfully aware that the endless hardships I suffer – starvation, cold, sleeping outdoors – have reduced me to the same wretched state as him; I hardly recognise the gaunt and wild-eyed creature that I've become, and on the rare occasions I encounter people, they avoid me like the plague. I have no one and nothing left in my life. No friends. No family. No hearth. No home. All that's left is the hatred that grows ever greater, even as my physical strength seeps slowly away.

You find me now stumbling across a vast expanse of ice, wrapped in furs and laden down with a pack. The harsh beauty of the Arctic is lost on me, for my heart has shrivelled and my soul's turned sour.

Instead, every bit of my attention is focussed on the trail of boot prints in the snow. They're so fresh! He cannot be far ahead now. In the distance I spy a bulky figure, bent against the wind. The creature turns and faces me. Perhaps he possesses some preternatural sense that alerts him to my presence...

"Monster! Fiend!" I bellow, shrugging off my pack and drawing my pistol with freezing fingers. "I promised to pursue you to the ends of the earth, and here I find you." I quicken my pace, desperate to close the gap before he can escape.

Still running, I aim my pistol and make ready to fire... and then I hear the most horrible sound I've ever heard in my life: the cracking of ice beneath my feet, and before I can even scream, it gives way and plunges me into the water.

Cold such as I've never felt before! Limbs instantly paralysed. Air frozen in my lungs. My pistol sinks into the abyss. Sunlight probes through the jagged hole above. Something blocks it. Strong fingers grasp my wrist, dragging me upwards, and suddenly I'm lying on my back, gasping and shivering.

The creature stares down at me, its face impassive. "Soon you will die, Frankenstein. The cold will reach your heart and stop its beat, and I will be here to watch."

"I suppose... you think... you've won, demon," I say through chattering teeth.

"I've robbed you of everything you love, reduced you to a state as pitiful as

mine, and orchestrated your lonely death out here in the bleakest wilderness on Earth." The creature smiles. "Yes, I have won."

From deep inside, cutting through all these months of grief, misery and pain, comes a long and genuine laugh. "How wrong you are!" I say when my mirth subsides.

The creature cocks its head. "How so?"

"All you have... in this world... is me. It's your hatred... and thirst for revenge... that drives you. It's what gives... your existence... its only meaning." I reach up and grab his collar with both hands. "Without me... you have nothing. You're alone." I fall back onto the ice and for the first time in what seems like an eternity, feel at peace. My breath's shallow. I can't feel my limbs. Death is close. But I am ready.

The creature laughs harshly, kneels beside me and draws a thick bundle of papers from his coat. "Do you recognise these? I took them from your laboratory."

Horror creeps over me. "My notes," I gasp. "My experiments."

"Indeed. Detailed enough for me to replicate your work and form for myself a mate." He draws close enough so that all I can see is his hideous face. "With whom I shall be happy. With whom I shall be fulfilled. With whom I shall *breed*."

"*No...*" I gasp.

"And in time," he continues, "using the longevity, superior strength and intellect you bestowed upon us, we will consume your human race and take this planet for ourselves. I promise you, Victor Frankenstein, that will be your only legacy."

The Birth of a Monster

Mary Wollstonecraft Shelley (1797–1851) was only eighteen years old when she wrote *Frankenstein*, her first and most famous novel. Dark and deeply shocking, this grisly Gothic horror story of an obsessed student bringing life to a corpse was an overnight sensation. People gleefully shared their copies of the book and stage adaptations were put on to sell-out crowds. Critics either loved or hated *Frankenstein* – but no one was indifferent to this young woman's tale of hubris, death and bloody revenge.

Tragedy was a constant grim companion during Mary Shelley's life. Her mother, a respected writer, philosopher and fierce advocate for woman's rights, died only days after giving birth to her. Her father, also a writer and philosopher, ensured Mary had a good education, and she grew up surrounded by some of the greatest thinkers of the age. All these influences inspired her to become a writer.

Mary was sixteen when she fell in love with Percy Bysshe Shelley, one of the most famous (and already married) poets of that time. Mary soon became pregnant and gave birth to a daughter in 1815. Sadly, her daughter

died only a few weeks later. Over the following years, Mary lost her half-sister to suicide, two more children when they were very young, and nearly perished herself from a miscarriage. All of this grief and death occurred before Mary had reached her mid-twenties; with a story centring on a man reanimating a corpse, it's impossible to imagine that these tragedies didn't influence Mary's writings.

In the summer of 1816, Mary, Percy and another poet, Lord Byron, were travelling together in Switzerland. One thundery night, Lord Byron suggested a competition to see who could come up with the most frightening story. Mary wracked her brains, but for several days could think of nothing suitable. Then, one sleepless night, from her fertile imagination a terrible vision appeared: "I saw the pale student of unhallowed arts kneeling beside the thing he had put together."

Mary turned her startling vision into a novel, and in 1818 *Frankenstein* hit the shelves. Fearful that people might be so shocked by her book's disturbing themes that they'd consider her an unfit mother, she decided to publish anonymously. Now, over 200 years later, Mary's creation is famous all over the world, and her contribution to horror literature as well as popular culture is assured.

Vasilisa the Daughter

Wouldst thou hear a tale of vengeance?
Wouldst thou hear a tale of blood?

I hold gently onto Mother's hand and let my tears pour upon it.

Fingers once long and shapely are broken and bent, each nail torn out, with bruises blooming 'neath the skin.

My mother's voice, once a balm and honey-sweet, croaks forth from swollen lips. "Vasilisa, I do love thee marvellous well."

I love thee too, I wish to reply, but the words lodge fast in my throat.

"My time is nigh," she saith from her bed of rotten straw, "and anon thou willst be alone in this cruel world. But know this: whatever happens, I will be smiling upon thee, watching and protecting thee from my place in Heaven."

A figure emerges from the shadows and into the lantern light. 'Tis the witch hunter! He, who with his knot of henchmen didst enter our village and visit upon us such persecution it didst turn our world upside down. He, who named my mother 'witch', he who forced a false confession, and he who sentenced her to death.

"Speak not Heaven's name with thy forked tongue," he saith, "and cast from thy worm-eaten mind all thoughts of ascension into God's grace."

"My mother ain't a witch!" I cry.

"Three witnesses spied her a-flying o'er the river, to consort with the Devil, who appeared to her in the form of a tar-black billy goat."

"They lied because they fear thee!"

"Water doesn't fear me, and water doesn't lie, and the whole village entire saw the river reject thy mother's corrupt form when we swam her in't."

"A trick! Thou held her aloft with the ropes."

"I'll have thee silent! Thou knowest naught of my methods."

I glare at him. "But I see how fat thy purse hath become, Witch Hunter, paid as thou art for every burning. Thou art like Judas, making profit from the death of innocent folk."

"Go to, wretch! I do God's work and I'll suffer not thy accusations." A vicious gleam kindles in his eyes and he points to the devious engine-of-pain-and-torment that lurks like a demon in the corner. "Or wouldst thou fancy a dalliance on the rack?"

"Nay, Witch Hunter," Mother saith with much anguish, "spare my daughter thy attention, I beg. She is a good girl!"

He inclines his head towards me. "Malapert Vasilisa may be, but I smell no witchery upon her."

"Oh, thank God..." Mother cries.

"And yet," he saith, brow knitted in thought, "now that I pore on't, I measure her more likely to fall into malefic ways, offspring as she is to a foul sorceress such as thee. I would be remiss in my duty if I didst naught to swerve her from this path."

Mother's eyes spread wide in their sockets. "What devilry dost thou intend?"

"No devilry," the knave returns. "That is *thy* domain. I merely intend to show thy daughter a witch's fate... by having her watch thee burn."

A gesture brings forth two henchmen, who drag my mother outside, past the baying mob and into the village square where a blackened stake awaits.

I watch, helpless, as they bind her, pile tinder round her feet and touch the torch to it; I weep as the first flames bite the fuel; I scream as the wind blows life into the pyre, and howl as mine mother lifts her head as a woman drowning in a yellow sea. Th' inferno rises, ravenous; sparks crackle 'mid greasy smoke, and I only close mine eyes when she's consumed entire and hath become a silent shadow within the blaze.

The witch hunter casts me aside and gathers his minions close. "Disperse this rabble then rest thyselves. Our labours in this pigsty continue in the morn."

My throat is raw, my eyes burn and my heart o'erflows with hate. I desire, from the depths of my agonised soul, vengeance upon he who hath torn my life asunder.

And so to the Greenwood, Vasilisa. To the witch.

I stand 'pon the edge of the Greenwood. Mist be-skirted trees loom afore me. Branches entwine o'er my head, knocking like bones in the wind. Within lives the witch, whose ancient name none 'cept me dare speak.

"Baba Yaga, Baba Yaga, I dost seek thy aid."

I straighten my spine and plunge into the shadows.

"Baba Yaga, Baba Yaga, I have flesh to trade."

Deeper, deeper, like an insect I creep.

"Baba Yaga, Baba Yaga, I beg help with my plan." Soon I am lost, but ever-forwards I go.

"Baba Yaga, Baba Yaga, I wish the death of a man."

'Tis nightfall when a black goose steps into my path, and with a flick of her wing bids me follow. She leads me to a glade fenced with bones, each topped with a glowing skull; toe-bone hinges creak as she pushes the gate. Ahead stands a house upon a pair of giant chicken legs with claws spread wide on the grass.

The goose gives a honk, the door opens and a ladder drops down. Up, up I climb, on shaking legs, into the witch's domain. 'Tis dark – the only glim cometh from an iron stove; a bubbling pot loads the air with fumes; ancient floorboards creak 'neath my feet.

"Prithee..." I quoth, then jump from my skin as the door behind me slams shut.

Straw rustles. Something heavy stirs the shadows. As mine eyes grow sharp 'gainst the gloom, I see a pair of filthy feet, big as dogs, behind me, a clawed hand splayed beside me, and two gleaming eyes afore me. 'Tis Baba Yaga, stretched out 'pon her side, bent like a serpent to encircle the room.

"What dost thou want, little morsel?" she saith in a voice grave-deep.

"Thou help, if it please thee."

"And what wouldst thou give me in kind?"

"Whatever thou desire."

"And what... if my desire... is THEE?" Baba Yaga thrusts her huge head into the light. "To eat of thy flesh, to gnaw on thy bones and set thy skull atop a fencepost to light my way in the dark?"

I drop to my knees, hold my clasped hands o'er my head and tell of my mother's fate.

The witch sheathes her iron teeth and returns to the dark. "Fain I would be to help thee, juicy bite, for thy mother's sake. I shall brew magic for thy purpose if thou bringst me what I need."

"Prithee tell, and I shall obey."

"Hist me first!" she saith, holding up a knobbly finger. "Sorcery demands sacrifice from whosoever casts it. Art thou willing to give of thyself?"

"Verily I am," I saith, most earnest and sincere.

"Very well. Yonside of the Greenwood – my goose will guide thee – lies a swamp lit by ghostlights. Within its dank waters leeches live. Bring me one hundred – no more, no less – and ensure they be fat with thy blood."

'Tis full dark when I begin my journey. The goose leadeth me, flapping with
ease o'er branches and brambles, while I blunder behind. We walk for what feels
like hours. At last, I emerge on the edge of a ghost-lit swamp. Mist swirls, frogs
creak, reeds rustle. The goose honks, and waits.

I lift up my skirts and wade into the swamp; the water is warm; the mire
swallows my feet. I need not wait long... Hither they come by the score... A fleet
of wriggling leeches... Converging upon me... Slithering silently o'er my skin...
Affixing their mouth-parts...

I return to the glade with my thirsty cargo. There Baba Yaga awaits,
towering o'er me, immense: an ancient idol, a primal force, a forest goddess.

"What went thou, greasy dumpling, out into the swamp to gather?"

"One hundred leeches."

"And didst thou find them?"

"Nay," I reply, lifting my skirts. "They found me."

"Then take this knife and fill yonder mortar with them."

The leeches by now art full and bloated, so I scrape them from my legs
and scoop them into the mortar. The witch looms behind me, teeth gnashing
and breathing hot 'pon my neck as I work.

"Thou must grind them till I stop thee. And if thou dost rest even just for a moment, I shall roast thee, my cutlet, and have thee for my supper."

So I set to my task with intent: mushing, grinding and pestling as the sun, moon and stars wheel thrice o'erhead. At last, Baba Yaga shouts "Stop!", drops a doll into the mortar and tarries till she's drunk every drop of the leechy paste.

"And now, my basted turtledove," she saith, passing me needle, thread and a bolt of black cloth, "I'll have thee make a costume for this malevolent poppet. Fail, and I shall gnaw slowly upon thee from toe to crown."

So, with heart a-pounding, I set about sewing britches, coat and hat like those worn by the witch hunter. The cloth's rough as oakum and doth rub my fingers so raw it becomes infused with my blood. I care not. Once done and dressed, Baba Yaga mutters magic-freighted words upon the poppet.

"The curse is complete," Baba Yaga saith at last. "And I am cheated of mine supper. Now, go thither and wreak thy revenge."

'Tis night in my village, and the witch hunter's plying his deadly trade afore a restive crowd. He paces like a wolf, face washed orange by the blazing torch in his hand; methinks I have arrived in the nick of time.

"Each day I tilt with Satan and bring his servants to the light," he cries, pointing to a raven-haired maiden tied to a stake behind him. "Behold this enchantress, this weaver of discord, who lurked within thy midst!"

And the people who I once called 'neighbour' cry, "Burn her alive!"

I worm my way through the maddened crowd, clutching the black-clad poppet, the vessel of my vengeance, tightly to my breast. I know exactly what actions are required of me, but naught of their culmination. And so, with my remit scored deep into my heart, I wait, breath held, as mine mortal enemy thrusts his torch into the tinder and stands back in satisfaction to watch his handiwork.

Smoke thickens. Flames feast and reach upwards towards the maiden's feet. With a prayer to mine mother 'pon my lips, I step forth and toss the poppet into the hottest part of the fire.

It shrivels and writhes. Little arms flail. Legs kick. The leech mush within hisses and turns to black steam. A sudden breeze springs up, whipping the flames into a raging inferno that engulfs the figure tied helpless to the stake. But afore it starts screaming, and its eyes melt, and its skin blackens, and its flesh bubbles off its bones, I behold its agonised face... and a smile creeps o'er my lips.

For the face be that of the witch hunter!

I turn my gaze to where he stood just a moment agone and see instead the raven-haired woman – 'mazed and unharmed – wearing the witch hunter's black britches, coat and hat. The crowd stare agog as mine enemy screams for mercy and struggles in vain in the fire of his own creation. The smell of roasting flesh fills my nose; peace born from vengeance fills mine heart.

I reach out and take the maiden's hand and lead her like a sister from this world of hate and accusation to the safety of my new domain: the Greenwood, home of the witches.

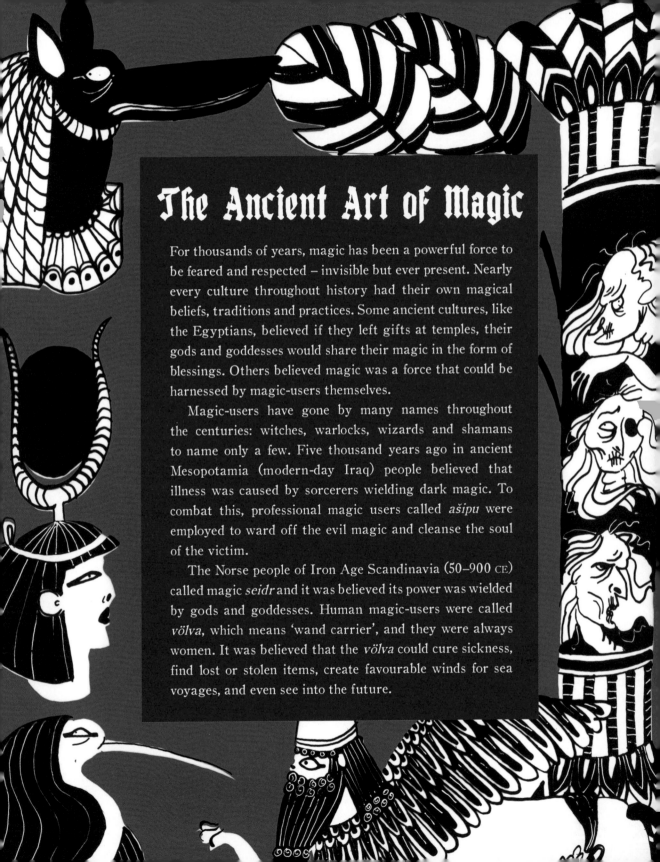

The Ancient Art of Magic

For thousands of years, magic has been a powerful force to be feared and respected – invisible but ever present. Nearly every culture throughout history had their own magical beliefs, traditions and practices. Some ancient cultures, like the Egyptians, believed if they left gifts at temples, their gods and goddesses would share their magic in the form of blessings. Others believed magic was a force that could be harnessed by magic-users themselves.

Magic-users have gone by many names throughout the centuries: witches, warlocks, wizards and shamans to name only a few. Five thousand years ago in ancient Mesopotamia (modern-day Iraq) people believed that illness was caused by sorcerers wielding dark magic. To combat this, professional magic users called *ašipu* were employed to ward off the evil magic and cleanse the soul of the victim.

The Norse people of Iron Age Scandinavia (50–900 CE) called magic *seidr* and it was believed its power was wielded by gods and goddesses. Human magic-users were called *völva*, which means 'wand carrier', and they were always women. It was believed that the *völva* could cure sickness, find lost or stolen items, create favourable winds for sea voyages, and even see into the future.

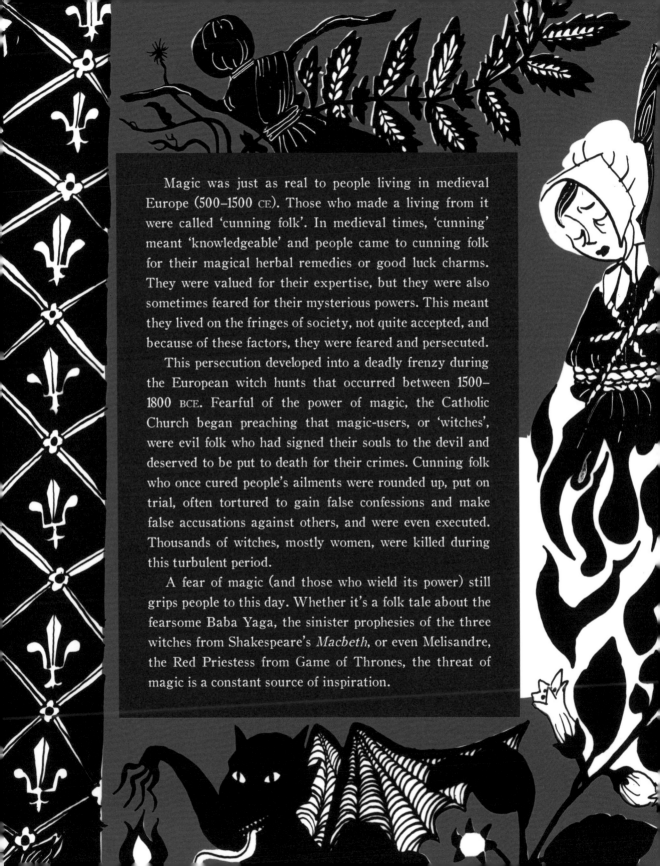

Magic was just as real to people living in medieval Europe (500–1500 CE). Those who made a living from it were called 'cunning folk'. In medieval times, 'cunning' meant 'knowledgeable' and people came to cunning folk for their magical herbal remedies or good luck charms. They were valued for their expertise, but they were also sometimes feared for their mysterious powers. This meant they lived on the fringes of society, not quite accepted, and because of these factors, they were feared and persecuted.

This persecution developed into a deadly frenzy during the European witch hunts that occurred between 1500–1800 BCE. Fearful of the power of magic, the Catholic Church began preaching that magic-users, or 'witches', were evil folk who had signed their souls to the devil and deserved to be put to death for their crimes. Cunning folk who once cured people's ailments were rounded up, put on trial, often tortured to gain false confessions and make false accusations against others, and were even executed. Thousands of witches, mostly women, were killed during this turbulent period.

A fear of magic (and those who wield its power) still grips people to this day. Whether it's a folk tale about the fearsome Baba Yaga, the sinister prophesies of the three witches from Shakespeare's *Macbeth*, or even Melisandre, the Red Priestess from Game of Thrones, the threat of magic is a constant source of inspiration.

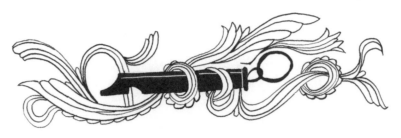

Whistle and I'll Come to You

Professor Parkin was only ever at ease when absorbed in a book on some dusty subject like archaeology, or on long walks in places where he was unlikely to meet other people.

It wasn't exactly that he didn't *like* people, he just found them... difficult. To talk to. To understand. If anyone tried to engage him in conversation, they always chose subjects like sport (in which he had no interest), the news (which he never followed) or the weather. And if Parkin introduced subjects he enjoyed, the conversation became a rather one-sided lecture, which caused the other party to glaze over until they invented an excuse to escape.

This ingrained awkwardness, coupled with an ambivalence towards 'making an effort' (something his mother – now deceased – had often begged of him) has ensured that Professor Parkin spent most of his fifty-six years alone. He eats alone, sleeps alone – he even holidays alone.

And this is where we find him: in a small seaside hotel, standing awkwardly in the lobby, wondering where the receptionist is, but not ringing the bell because to do so seemed rude.

"Er, I say... Hello?" he said at a volume he hoped wasn't too loud to disturb anyone. "Is there someone about?"

After a minute or two a young woman emerged and hurried behind the reception desk. "Sorry to keep you waiting, " she said. "Could I have your name?"

"It's Parkin. Professor Parkin. I telephoned, oh, a week ago, I suppose it was, to reserve a room."

"Ah, yes, here we are... Room 8. If you'd like to follow me?"

Parkin creaked up the stairs behind her; the silence made him uncomfortable, but he could think of nothing to say so he just hummed under his breath.

The room was pleasant (although Parkin noted with mild surprise that it had two beds) and the day was still young, so after unpacking his clothes (sturdy, practical, old-fashioned) and books (obscure Sumerian deities and demons), he decided to take a turn along the beach.

An hour or so later, Parkin was striding along a wide stretch of firm, flat sand, swinging his walking stick and relishing the salty air. Inland, to his left, the beach rose into a riddle of dunes. Long grass rustled there. Sand hissed. On his right, nibbling at the beach, the grey and restless sea.

He was entirely alone – his were the only footprints – and the hotel was far behind and long out of sight. Parkin wondered if this was the scene beheld by the first humans when they arrived on these shores ten thousand years ago.

A university colleague had told him he might find the ruins of a 13th century Knights Templar church in this part of the world, and when Parkin spied crooked gravestones and hummocks of flint-studded masonry sticking out of the ground, he went to have a look.

Ah yes, there the foundations of a round tower, a narrow portal, an alter... Parkin's own research had informed him the knights had built this church on a far older burial site, and he wondered what Pagan artefacts lay buried under his feet.

After a bit more poking around he decided to head back. As he clambered down to the beach he noticed a thin, cigar-shaped object sticking out of the ground.

Curious, he picked it up and put it in his pocket.

"Examine that later," he muttered.

Dusk – that strange, murky, liminal part of the day – had fallen by the time he was once again scrunching across the sand. The sea was closer, the wind cold, the sky sullen and low. Parkin was looking forward to supper and a good read before bed, and apart from having to clamber over wooden wall-like groynes every now and again, he made good progress.

He turned to measure how far he'd walked and was surprised to see in the distance an indistinct figure. The dim light made it hard to be sure, but Parkin had the distinct impression it was running to catch up with him, yet at the same time not making any actual progress.

Most odd.

Parkin briefly considered waiting on the personage, but – and I'm sure this will not surprise you, knowing as you now do a bit about his character – decided instead to continue alone.

Later that evening, Parkin enjoyed supper at a table in the corner of the dining room before retiring to bed. He was just laying out his jacket when the object he'd found fell from the pocket.

"Well, well," he said. "I'd forgotten about you."

He took it to the desk and examined it under the light. After rubbing off several layers of grime he realised it was a whistle made from bone, and obviously very old. His interest was piqued further when he saw it was inscribed with marks – and not just marks, but *letters*.

Parkin scraped the dirt from each groove, then copied the letters onto a notepad:

QUIS EST ISTE QUI VENIT

"My Latin's a bit rusty," he murmured. "But I think I can..." Frowning with concentration, Parkin wrote down his best attempt at a translation, then stared with an almost unconscious disquiet at the resulting sentence.

"Who is this... that is coming? I wonder what that means." He picked up the whistle and turned it over in his hands. "Perhaps I should give it a try and find out."

Parkin put the whistle to his lips and blew; the note that emerged was clear, and although quiet gave the impression it could be heard for many miles around. It also, much to his surprise, created a vivid image in his mind of a wide beach, and in the centre a distant and solitary figure; the image disappeared as a sudden gust of wind howled around the eaves and rattled the windows.

A person of more imagination than our Professor Parkin might have found that disconcerting, but he was a deeply rational man. That said, he did pass a rather uncomfortable night, drifting in a space somewhere between wakefulness and dream, and occasionally disturbed by the sound of rustling bedsheets.

The bright morning sun and the prospect of breakfast revived Parkin's energy with miraculous speed, and he was the first in the dining room to enjoy grapefruit and toast. Indeed, his mood was so improved he decided to risk reading in one of the common rooms, rather than the privacy of his own room.

Other guests came and went, hefting golf bags (there was an excellent club nearby), chatting about their plans for the day and generally taking no notice of the quiet man sitting in the corner with his nose buried in a book. Until, that is, a bespeckled woman plonked herself down on a chair opposite.

"On your own again?" she said.

Parkin looked up, nonplussed by this sudden ambush. "I beg your pardon?"

"I saw you at breakfast this morning. You not here with anybody?"

"No," Parkin replied. "I'm quite alone, thank you."

"Aw, shame," she said sympathetically. "Me and my husband are heading into town to do some shopping. Would you like to join us?"

"That's most kind," Parkin (who could think of nothing worse than shopping with strangers) said, "but I'm going for a trudge along the beach this afternoon."

"But there's nothing there?" the woman frowned. "No cafés or anything?"

"Oh, there's plenty around if you know where to look. Indeed, I stumbled upon a ruined church on my wanderings yesterday."

"Ruined church? Sounds spooky."

Parkin's eyes narrowed. "Spooky?"

"Yes. Ghosts, restless spirits. Don't you believe in that sort of thing?"

"Well, why on Earth would I?" he said, adopting the tone he took with his most difficult students. "Why would you? Why would *anyone* believe in things without any empirical evidence to prove their existence? Why cling to the superstitions of our ancestors when we now live in a brave new age of science and technology, discovery and advancement, progress and invention?"

"I'm not clinging to superstitions," the woman said, taken aback. "I'm just saying that some places have a certain – oh, I don't know – atmosphere."

"Spooky. *Atmosphere.*" Parkin gave a condescending chuckle. "None of these things can be grasped in the hand, can they? Or viewed under a microscope? Indeed, if you asked ten people to define those words, you'd get thirty different answers. Take my advice, madam, and discard such worthless notions."

Good deed for the day thoroughly thwarted, and feeling both confused and offended, the woman retreated, leaving Parkin alone to finish his chapter in peace.

Supper consumed and with another long walk under his belt, a tired Parkin went to bed. And yet, instead of drifting off to sleep when he closed his eyes, he was confronted with another vision, playing out like a film in his mind: a wide and empty beach, intersected with dark wooden groynes running down to a listless sea. In the distance a man, running, stumbling, clambering in the manner of someone terrified. Every few moments he glances over his shoulder, then plunges onward, although it was clear to Parkin that he was nearly at the end of his strength.

Behind him but getting ever closer, another figure: pale, hard to define in the grey light, and possessing an odd, fluttery outline, like an empty robe caught in a breeze. There was something about its stooped posture and rapid, predatory movements that chilled Parkin to his bones.

The man threw himself over the nearest groyne and cowered at its base, staring up, waiting, as the pale figure on the other side paused, turned in his direction, threw up its arms and fluttered straight towards him.

It was at this point that Parkin's courage deserted him and he opened his eyes. After enduring this torment several times (as well as the sound of rustling sheets from somewhere or other), he decided enough was enough, turned on the light and spent the rest of the night reading, but taking in not a single word.

"Which bed would you like the extra blanket on, sir?" a maid asked Parkin as he emerged, towelling his face, from the bathroom the next morning.

"Which bed?" he echoed. "Why, the one I slept in, of course."

"Pardon me, sir, but it looks like you gave both a try."

Parkin drifted his tired eyes over both beds and saw she was right – the covers of the one he didn't use were as jumbled and tangled as the one he did.

"Strange," he muttered. "I must have disturbed them somehow."

After breakfast, Parkin felt an unusual craving to be around people, so he went into town, wandered around shops, had tea in a café and visited a museum. There were lots of people about, but proximity is not the same as intimacy, and strangers are not the same as friends, and when Parkin returned to the hotel he was aware of a dull emptiness in his stomach to which he couldn't attach a reason.

Actually, it was loneliness, pure and simple.

He surprised himself when he tried to strike up a conversation with the bespeckled woman, but she was clearly still smarting from their previous encounter and gave him short shrift. As daylight faded, and bedtime neared, Parkin's loneliness changed to unease, and finally to dread.

He thought of the whistle, and the words scored onto its surface.

WHO IS THIS, THAT IS COMING?

He stayed in the common room, taking as much comfort as he could from being near the other guests until, one by one, they all retired to their rooms. Eventually, giving in to the inevitable, he ascended the stairs, changed into his pyjamas, slipped into bed and turned out the light. It took courage just to close his eyes, but to his relief the vision of the beach did not return.

However, the soft rustling of sheets did, and for the first time he realised the sound was coming from the other bed. Parkin peered into the darkness.

"Is... is anyone there?"

The only answer was the gentle swish and slide of layers of cotton rubbing together. Parkin fumbled for the light, nearly knocking it over in his haste.

Had it been waiting, or was it stirred by the light? Who knows. But at that moment there rose from the bed – the bed that Parkin knew was empty – a pale and fluttering figure. Tall enough nearly to reach the ceiling, it bent over the professor and glared down at him with a hideous face of crumpled linen.

Mind broken, defences long-prepared shattered in an instant, Professor Parkin began to scream in terror.

Minutes later, the manager burst into the bedroom and beheld Professor Parkin sitting on his bed, knees drawn up to his chin, shaking and cowering in front of at an empty pile of sheets on the floor.

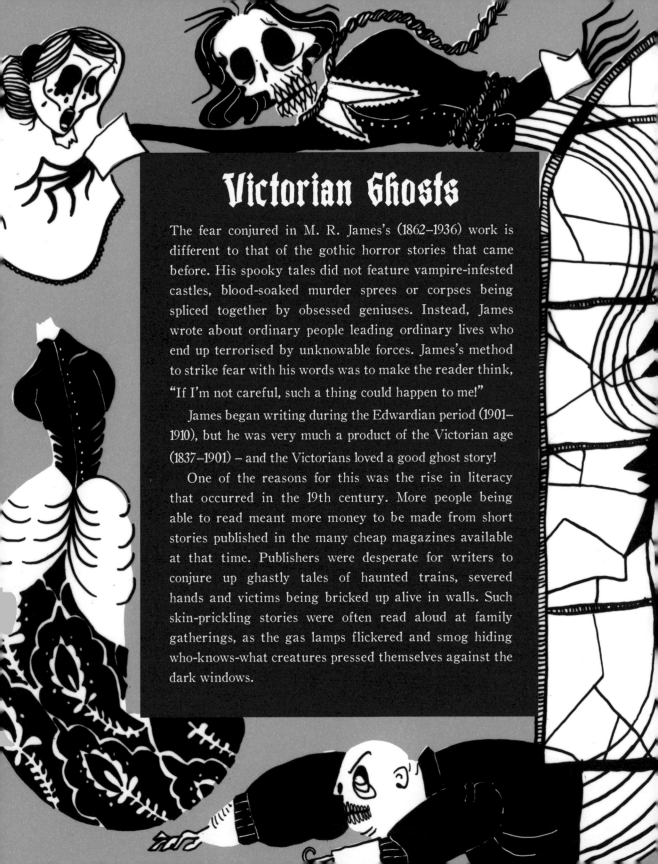

Victorian Ghosts

The fear conjured in M. R. James's (1862–1936) work is different to that of the gothic horror stories that came before. His spooky tales did not feature vampire-infested castles, blood-soaked murder sprees or corpses being spliced together by obsessed geniuses. Instead, James wrote about ordinary people leading ordinary lives who end up terrorised by unknowable forces. James's method to strike fear with his words was to make the reader think, "If I'm not careful, such a thing could happen to me!"

James began writing during the Edwardian period (1901–1910), but he was very much a product of the Victorian age (1837–1901) – and the Victorians loved a good ghost story!

One of the reasons for this was the rise in literacy that occurred in the 19th century. More people being able to read meant more money to be made from short stories published in the many cheap magazines available at that time. Publishers were desperate for writers to conjure up ghastly tales of haunted trains, severed hands and victims being bricked up alive in walls. Such skin-prickling stories were often read aloud at family gatherings, as the gas lamps flickered and smog hiding who-knows-what creatures pressed themselves against the dark windows.

Another reason was that death itself was a Victorian obsession. This was led by Queen Victoria, who began a long period of mourning when her husband, Prince Albert, died in 1861. It was a loss from which she never recovered: she wore black for the rest of her days and retreated from public life. Driven by this behaviour, a formal etiquette around death arose. Widows wore black for two years, clocks were stopped after a death and mirrors were covered to prevent the deceased's image getting trapped in the glass. It became customary to have photographs taken of the corpse, often propped up in a chair, surrounded by their living family members.

This obsession fuelled a rise in spiritualism. Many people attended seances, where spiritualists claimed to use powers to contact the dead. The movement began in the United States in the mid 19th century, when sisters Margaretta and Catherine Fox said they could induce the dead to speak from beyond the grave. Communication came in the form of loud 'rapping' sounds, and for a while the sisters made a good living – until they were exposed as fakes. No matter. Seances became big business throughout the US and Europe, and people paid lots of money to speak to those they'd lost.

All these factors helped create the Victorian appetite for stories of ghosts, ghouls and spooky encounters on lonely Suffolk beaches...

Bluebeard

Not far from here lived a high-spirited young woman called Maeve. Everybody loved her for her warm and kindly heart. One day, a rich man called Bluebeard visited her village. Everyone was afraid of Bluebeard, because his bulging eyes, bushy beard and the sword on his hip made him look quite ferocious – not to mention the rumours about his previous wives.

But Maeve saw past these things, judged Bluebeard to be charming and warm, and soon fell in love with the man before her. He was kind, gentle and attentive to her needs, and after a joyous wedding Bluebeard whisked Maeve far away to his castle where he showered her with affections.

But one evening at supper, when Meave was about to eat a slice of cake, Bluebeard frowned and said, "I don't think you should have any pudding. You might get too fat for the dresses I've bought you."

Maeve was shocked and a little hurt. But she owed everything to Bluebeard, so did as she was told and pushed the plate away. Her husband smiled and set about his own cake with gusto. Meave put this to the back of her mind.

One week later, Maeve was at her dressing table deciding how to wear her hair. "I shall have it down today, to flow freely around my shoulders," she thought.

Bluebeard appeared behind her and piled her golden tresses upon the top of her head. "I want you to pin your hair up like this from now on," he said sternly.

"But it's my hair," Maeve replied. "Can I not wear it as I please?"

"I didn't realise my new wife was so *selfish*," Bluebeard said. "Do you not want to make your husband happy?"

Indeed she did, so from then on she wore her hair just as Bluebeard wanted.

Maeve often felt lonely rattling around the castle on her own, so she told Bluebeard she wanted to visit her friends and family. But Bluebeard shook his shaggy head.

"I've heard tell that those you love have grown resentful of your new wealth and fortune," he said. "You won't be welcome in your village, so you must stay here with me."

"I cannot believe those I hold most dear would ever wish me ill," Maeve said, distraught at the idea.

"But I know better than you the cruelties of this world," Bluebeard explained, "and how the worst betrayals come from those we thought closest to us. They hate you now, and it's best you don't see them ever again."

And so, with a heavy heart, Maeve agreed.

A week later Maeve went for a walk beyond the castle walls. The birdsong, breeze and bright blue sky lifted her spirits, and she returned home happy. But inside Bluebeard was waiting for her.

"The land beyond my walls is dangerous," he said, "and I forbid you to go there ever again."

"But I can look after myself perfectly well," Maeve replied.

"No, you can't. You're weak and need me to protect you." Bluebeard wagged his finger at her. "And do not think of disobeying me on this or any other matter. Remember, my servants report to me your every move."

After that, Maeve felt lonelier than ever before.

To celebrate one year of marriage, Bluebeard threw a party for his friends. Maeve mingled and laughed with his guests, glad to have some company for once. When everyone had gone Maeve retired to her bedchamber. Bluebeard burst in as Maeve was taking off her shoes.

"How *dare* you embarrass me like that?" he thundered. "Have you no shame?"

"My husband, beloved, whatever do you mean?" she asked.

"Don't play innocent with me," he said. "I saw you seducing all the men!"

"Indeed I was not," she replied. "I was merely trying to be a good hostess."

Bristling with untrammelled rage Bluebeard shouted, "You were flaunting yourself like a dog in heat," and he shoved her against the bed.

Maeve ran away and listened in terror as Bluebeard bellowed, raged and cursed her name. After a while, the castle grew quiet. Maeve emerged from her hiding place and went to find her husband.

"My precious wife," Bluebeard said when she found him, "I'm truly sorry, and promise never to hurt you again. Do you forgive me?"

And Maeve, possessed of a warm and kindly heart, said, "I do, dear husband, for we all make mistakes."

Bluebeard sighed and enveloped Maeve in his arms. "Thank you," he said. "But you must accept your share of the blame and promise never to provoke me to violence again." And so, just to put that dreadful night behind her, Maeve made the promise.

Weeks passed, during which Bluebeard was more like the man Maeve had fallen for. One day he said, "I must leave for a while on business, and for your own protection I forbid you from stepping foot outside."

Maeve glanced mournfully through the barred windows at the sunny skies beyond. "But surely I'll be safe in the castle grounds?"

Bluebeard stood up, casting his shadow over her. "I *hope* you're not about to break your promise and provoke me."

Remembering the feeling of shock and fear from that night, Maeve looked down and replied, "No, dear husband. I shall keep my promise."

"Good," Bluebeard nodded. "Now, take this key. It will open all the doors inside my castle. However, you must not enter the room in the north tower. There is nothing for you in there." And with that final warning he left, locking the castle gate behind him.

Like a trapped cat, Maeve wandered the corridors until she found herself standing by the forbidden door. "I do so wish to feel the sun on my face," she thought. "Perhaps this portal leads to the garden." And so, drawing on her last remaining scrap of independence, Maeve unlocked the door.

Beyond lay a staircase leading down into the dark. At the bottom Maeve found a chamber. First she saw the hooks, knives and cleavers strewn upon a table; then the lake of clotted blood lapping around her ankles; and finally the four severed heads hanging by their hair from the walls.

    As Maeve stared at their bloated faces, maggot-filled mouths and mildewed skin, she realised these must be Bluebeard's previous wives, and that she was bound to face an identical fate. Quaking with fear, Maeve stumbled up the steps with but one thought in mind: *escape*!

Maeve's heart nearly stopped when she reached the top and heard the castle gate open. Bluebeard called out, "Good tidings – my business is concluded and I have returned early!" and his heavy footsteps grew steadily closer.

Maeve stared in horror at the gory trail left on the flagstones by her blood-soaked shoes and dress. "When he sees me like this he'll know where I've been, and strike off my head with his sword," she thought.

"Where are you, wife?" Bluebeard said from the next room – and Maeve knew there was no escape.

"Beloved husband," Maeve cried, trying to steady herself. "How glad I am to hear your voice! Will you indulge me by closing your eyes?"

"Whatever for?"

"Because I have a surprise for you. Are they closed?"

"Yes, wife."

"Promise?"

"I promise."

Still spreading blood from her skirts, Maeve entered the next room and approached her husband. She drew Bluebeard to the window and, using her nimble fingers, gently tied his beard tightly to the bars. Then she stepped away and said, "You can open your eyes now."

Bluebeard did so, and upon seeing his crimson-covered wife, drew his sword and lunged towards her with wild eyes – but the knots in his beard held him fast. As he howled and bellowed and raged, Maeve drew herself up to her full height and fled from the castle.

With his murderous secret now exposed, Bluebeard tried to run away. But Maeve and the authorities soon hunted him down and locked him away. Bluebeard would never hurt anyone again. Maeve moved her family into the castle, and they filled it with so much life and light and laughter that she soon forgot about the horrors of her life with Bluebeard and the secret of his bloody chamber.

Blood, Guts and Gore

Bluebeard is very different to most of the other horror stories in this book. There's no magic, no mythical creatures, and although it features a terrifying monster, this is no ravening beast of the forest – all slavering jaws and slicing claws. The monster in this tale is *real*. He's an ordinary man who, after charming his way into several women's hearts, murders them and hangs their corpses on hooks. The fear evoked for hundreds of years by this tale is especially potent because of the believability of Bluebeard's character and actions – and the shocking reveal of his true nature when his wife ventures down into his killing room and discovers his blood-drenched secret...

Fairy tales – especially the older versions – are often violent, but nothing in them matches the sheer visual horror of Bluebeard's despicable work: the corpses strung up by the hair and the crimson lake of blood that laps around his new wife's feet. The gore in this scene evokes a physical response from the reader rather than a mental one: a visceral disgust in the pit our stomachs; indeed, the word 'visceral' comes from 'viscera', which means 'internal organs', and 'intestines' in particular.

Blood and gore are not essential requirements to make a horror story frightening. Oftentimes, the human imagination will craft far more disturbing visions when fed *less* information – the horror of the unknown nearly always outweighs something in light's full glare. However, the shock value of a severed limb, an arterial spray; or intestines spilling from a split abdomen can, when timed correctly, provide real shock value. The appeal of blood and gore in the horror genre lies in its ability to provoke such a strong, immediate reaction from its audience.

Bram Stoker's *Dracula* has its fair share of blood and gore. And as a novel about a blood-sucking vampire, it would be disappointing if it *didn't* contain any reference to his favoured beverage. However, it was Stoker's vivid description of Dracula after he's fed, with his bloated face and gore-slicked skin, and scenes of stakes being hammer-driven into chests and issuing forth fountains of foaming blood that were so shocking for audiences at the time. Shocking, but hugely *popular*...

Whether it comes in a novel, film, TV show, short story or video game, horror fans always crave the shock factor. From the bloody violence of Red Riding Hood, the baroque murders of Hannibal Lecter or the shambling Necromorphs on board the doomed spaceship *Ishimora* in the Dead Space video games, there's no lack of audience in the splatter-filled theatre of blood and gore.